Sas-squash

Sas-squash

BY **EZEKIEL WINFIELD**

STONE Pulp Press
STONEPULP.COM

Dedicated to the victims of The Squatch Wars.

Disclaimer: Everything in this story is true (except for this statement). Some names have been changed (nicknames have not). All scientific facts have been verified via YouTube and The History Channel.

Chapter 1

It was a new moon—not that it mattered; the heavy canopy of trees would have stolen even a full moon's light. The dying campfire provided minimal luminance for Garret Petric and Davis Dugger, who sat outside their tent, lobbing emptied beer cans into the fire's coals.

Duggar said, "You seriously don't think *Braveheart* is a good movie?"

"I didn't say that," Garret said. "I said it is overrated."

"But it's like the greatest movie of all time."

"No, it's an adequate execution of a few historically inaccurate battle scenes—" he shifted in his seat to better argue his point, "—which, by the way, I don't know why they didn't just recreate the actual battles, seeing as the real ones are a hundred times more compelling."

"So you don't think it is one of the greatest movies of all time?"

"I just said that."

"But it's so great."

"It's good."

"But you just said it's not good."

"Look, are you listening to me? It's a good movie. But it's overrated. It's not a *great* movie. Outside of a few solid battle scenes, it's boring and not even remotely accurate. It was nothing more than an ego project for its star, who was clearly working out some deep-seated personal demons, and people who say otherwise don't know any better."

"Boring? How can you say it's boring?"

"Besides the battles, name one compelling scene in the movie."

Dugger looked at the dying fire and bobbed his head in the childlike shrug he defaulted to when backed into a logic corner. "I don't know," he said, saying it so quickly he turned the phrase into a single word—*Idunno*. "The love story is good."

Garret snorted. "The only reason you remember the love story is because the girls were hot. And that isn't an accident, by the way. The reason they put those girls in in the first place is to distract from the fact that the movie is actually gay porn. It's gay porn for straight guys—or at least guys who think they're straight. All that bloodlust is a metaphor for the struggle manly dudes have, but won't admit to having: the struggle against their own latent homosexuality."

"What the hell are you talking about?"

"All the violence is basically gay rape fantasy."

"You're crazy."

"Name the most violent scene."

Dugger looked off at the fire again. "Idunno," he said, thinking. "When he smashes the guy in the face with the ball and chain?"

"Yeah, which happens when Wallace bursts into the guy's *bed*room in the middle of the night and smashes the guy's face with his dangling balls."

"Ball," Dugger corrected.

"Same thing. It was a pendulous phallus," Garret said. "Hell, even the movie's love scenes with the women are just ways for Wallace to rape the men ruling those women's lives. His bride's father. The princess's father-in-law—the princess was even acting as an extension *of* the king when Wallace fucks her, so he is actually fucking the king. And Wallace's bride having her throat cut, so she could no longer speak? That's Gibson's way of silencing females from his life. Again, a man trying to deal with his own fucked up feelings about women."

"At least he didn't call her sugar tits."

"Ha. I wonder if that would be anachronistic?" He shrugged and said, "We know she wasn't Jewish."

"I don't know what you're even talking about now," Dugger said.

Garret continued, as if unaware of his non sequitur. "And don't even get me started on the projective symbolism—pun intended—of Longshanks throwing his son's gay lover out the window. *Longshanks*," Garret snorted. "Dude's name is actually *Longshanks*. Sounds like a porn star." His voice lowered an octave. "Hi, my name is Vincenzo Longshanks, star of *Beefcake Bukake*."

"I think his name was really Longshanks. The king. I mean, in real life."

"That's not the point. The point is the love story of which you speak had nothing to do with the women in that movie. The love story is between Wallace and his men. Dudes, who don't recognize their own swelling feelings while watching it, think the theme of the movie is camaraderie with other dudes, but it's not. The theme is: I'm gay and don't know how to deal with it, so I will brutally kill a bunch of people. Look at the end of the movie, what happens?"

"They torture him to death?"

"Yeah, specifically they emasculate Wallace and disembowel him, i.e., they remove his penis and colon, otherwise known as his cock and asshole, a metaphor for the guilt of Gibson's latent homosexuality."

"But that really happened historically."

"Yeah, and *that's* the one historical accuracy Gibson decides to keep?"

"I really wish you hadn't become a psychology major."

"Me too."

"So you're saying that because I like that movie, I have latent homosexual tendencies?"

"Not necessarily. Look, there are two types of people who say *Braveheart* is their favorite movie. Those who actually believe it—you know the type: overcompensating tough guys born a few decades too late to have *Spartacus* usher them through their hidden homosexual feelings—and those who say it is their favorite movie because they can't *recognize* a great movie. So they use *Braveheart* because they're afraid saying another movie will make them look like a pussy. People like that aren't smart enough to just say *The Godfather* is their favorite movie. You, I think, fall into that category. So a word of advice: when someone asks your favorite movie, from now on tell them it's *The Godfather*."

"*The Godfather* is boring."

"Now you're just being a dick."

"So what's your favorite movie?"

"*The Cannonball Run*."

"That dumb car race movie?"

"*Cannonball's* simple stupidity is a thing of beauty."

"That's ridic—did you hear that?"

"Hear what?"

"Nothing, must be—what the fuck?" Dugger squealed as arms wrapped around his throat. A growl, like someone pretending to be a bear, was followed by laughter as J.J. Jenaway released Dugger and grabbed an unopened beer from the cooler. "What're you fags up to?" J.J. said.

Dugger flinched. "Dude, I don't think you can use that word anymore."

"What? Fag? Why not?"

"It's like derogatory or something. Ever notice in the TV edit of *A Few Good Men*, Jessup says 'girly white uniform,' instead of 'faggity white uniform'?"

"Wouldn't girly white uniform offend a higher percentage of the population?" Garret said.

"I don't know," Dugger said. "I just know you can't say fag anymore."

"That's retarded."

"I don't think you can say that either."

"Seriously?"

"Yeah. It's like using the n-word."

"Wait, you can't use the n-word anymore either?" J.J. said.

"I don't think you could ever use that one," Garret said.

"That's gay," J.J. said.

Dugger threw his hands in the air.

"It's like he's playing P.C. Bingo," Garret said.

"So where's Nick the Stick?" J.J. asked Dugger.

"I think he's in the chicks' tent banging Debbie," Dugger said.

"Where's the other chicks?"

"Getting banged in other tents."

"Why am I here with you two?" Garret growled.

"Good question," J.J. said. "I often wonder why you are invited along anywhere."

"That's what happens when you go camping with an odd number of chicks and dudes," Dugger said.

"Don't think it matters in your case…fag," J.J. said.

"Jesus, will you stop using—what is that sound?"

All three of them cocked their heads, listening.

J.J. said, "Sounds like…Debbie getting plowed."

"Bad idea," Garret said.

"What is?" Dugger said.

"Getting laid in the middle of nowhere on a creepy night? Seems rife for a horror trope."

"I suppose you two virgin losers are safe then," J.J said.

"And you, being the loud-mouth asshole, are not," Garret said.

"Only danger is the smell of all that jizz bringing bears," J.J. said.

"I don't think that sound is Debbie," Dugger said.

"Where have you been for the past hour anyway?" Garret asked J.J.

"Taking a shit."

"Won't that attract bears?"

"Why would shit attract them?"

"Because you took their job."

"Huh?" J.J. scrunched up his face. "A bear's job is shitting in the woods? I don't get it."

Dugger said, "Seriously, what is that sound?"

They stopped and cocked their heads again.

"I told you," J.J. said, "that's Debbie."

They cocked their heads one more time. There was the distinct sound of a girl moaning to the rhythm of her partner's thrusts, but there was another sound overlaying it, keeping the same rhythm, but this sound was almost inhuman—somehow high-pitched and low at the same time.

J.J. laughed, saying, "Damn, is that Nick? What the fuck is wrong with him?"

Garret said, "Judging from the duration of Debbie's moaning, nothing."

"No," Dugger said, "it doesn't sound like it's coming from the tents…I don't know, maybe it's coming from the trees?" He looked up toward the dark canopy of branches above them.

"Probably an echo or something," Garret said.

Dugger darted into a tent.

"Where's he going?" J.J. said.

"Probably to hide like the pussy he is?" Garret said. "After all, he did say *Braveheart* is his favorite movie."

"Great fucking movie," J.J. said.

Dugger returned with a flashlight and clicked it on, directing the beam upward like an air raid spotlight. The branches seemed to move and twine together in the movement of the light's beam, and then the light stopped and stayed on a figure in the canopy.

All three men spoke at once. Garret said, "Is that a man?" Dugger said, "Is that a bear?" J.J. said, "Think we'll see Debbie's tits?" He then looked at the thing in the tree and said, "Wait, is that a monkey?"

The thing in the tree looked like all of these things (aside from Debbie's tits). It looked like a giant gorilla, but lighter in color, almost blond. Its legs were long and sturdy, more like a man's. And it was the size of a bear. And…

"It has a mullet," J.J. said.

The thing had a flowing cascade of hair, which appeared to be crudely shorn into a mullet. The thing slapped its chest twice and raised its hands to its ears as if creating wings beside its head.

"Did he just do the—holy—" Dugger was cut off when the thing launched from the tree in a belly-flop motion. Twisting in the air to point its elbow downward, it crashed into Nick and Debbie's tent. With a sound like a faggot of sticks snapping, Debbie's rhythmic moaning went silent.

The thing that had plunged from the tree, leapt off the tent, and ran into the dark of night.

Other campers began climbing from their tents, pulling on clothing as they came.

The tangle of tent that housed Nick and Debbie was still for a moment, but then, like a fish in a net, something flailed inside the tangled nylon. No one thought to go to the tent to help. Everyone stood, gaping, as a delicate hand sprung from the nylon. The hand was followed by the nude body of Debbie Dobberman. She lurched and stumbled, gurgling blood. Ribs on the left side of her body poked from her flesh like a hand, the digits skewering her left breast. Her right breast was still pristine, and that's what Garret, Dugger, and J.J. focused on. Despite the carnage of her body, all the males in the campsite could focus only on that one perfect breast.

Mindy Robbins let out a scream, which finally broke Garret from his tit-nosis, and he ran to the crushed tent as Debbie collapsed. Ignoring the girl at his feet, he peeked into the tent. Nick the Stick was bent at all wrong angles. His face was implanted about an inch into the ground, while his still erect penis pointed north as a compass. "Whoa," Garret said. He turned to the gathering crowd around him. "That's fucked up."

Mindy fainted. Kyle Carter puked. J.J. still stared at Debbie's tit. But Dugger watched the dark of the forest as something moved about in the night. He caught glimpses of what looked like the giant monkey-man as it loped from tree to tree, seeming to bounce off each trunk to gain momentum, then suddenly launching through the campsite. It caught Kyle with a shoulder that bent him in half, and then a hand-plant to Garret's chest, which launched him back ten feet, and then a forearm to J.J.'s face, which literally knocked his head from his torso.

Dugger watched as J.J.'s decapitated head rolled and nestled inches from Debbie's right breast. J.J.'s eyes focused on that one perfect tit as the life left his eyes. Dugger then looked up and saw a wall of hair coming his way.

Chapter 2

Sheriff Malcolm Vance already recognized this whole ordeal as a good old fashion shitshow. Tall and stately, nearly everyone who met Vance thought he looked like Denzel Washington. Sounded like him too. He stood behind his desk with his hat cocked low on his head, hip tilted, right hand resting on the grip of his low-holstered .357 Magnum. The shitshow: a bunch of rich college kids—one of whom was the son of a senator—got killed by a bear, and now a bunch of "experts" were on their way, all because one of the survivors claimed it was a goddamn Bigfoot that did it.

Deputy Dan Dibble burst into the office. "First expert is here, Sheriff."

"Expert," the sheriff scoffed. "Right." He didn't move, just stood there with his hand on the butt of his revolver.

The deputy removed his hat and ran his hand over his peach-fuzz blond hair, a habit he was known to do when unsure of something—which was quite often. "Don'tcha want to meet her?"

"Her?"

"Yeah, it's a her. Said she was a prim…primer… prima tologist, so I'm guessing she's pretty good."

"Why would they send a primatologist?"

"I think it's pronounced *pree-ma*. And I just said why. I think prima means good. You know, like ballet? Or is that primo?"

The sheriff eyed his deputy, but didn't say a word. He left his spot behind his desk and stepped out his office door.

Outside his office was exactly what he expected. A shitshow. The ringing phones were a wall of noise, like a PBS telethon. The sheriff had to connect three extra phone lines and employ volunteers from around town—mostly retired switchboard operators, who weren't entirely sure how to work a phone without a rotary dial. Post-it notes covered the tables like a thin dusting of snow.

The sheriff regarded the bustle of people and mimicked his deputy's habit of removing his hat and running his hand over his head.

Deputy Dibble was beside him and said, "There she is, Sheriff." He pointed to a woman sitting in the corner. The woman was beautiful. Dark hair, shoulder length, eyes as green as a cliché.

The sheriff said, "Maybe primo *is* the right word." He removed his hat and walked to the woman, saying, "I'm Sheriff Malc—" but before he could finish, a man darted between them.

"Sheriff, Trent Tanner from the *Tribeca Tribune*. Is the creature really a Bigfoot, or is there an outbreak of rabid bears the citizens need to be aware of?"

The sheriff returned his hat to his head. "Hey, Trent," he said. "Nice to see you still not tripping over that alliterated intro. The official position of this office to your question is—" The sheriff placed his hands on the sides of Trent's arms and shuffled him off to the side. "Thanks, Trent." He then returned his attention to the woman, removing his hat again. "I'm Sheriff Malcolm Vance."

The woman didn't respond. Instead, she stared at Trent Tanner, saying, "*The Tribune*?"

Trent glanced at the woman and then darted his eyes away.

Sheriff Vance said, "I wouldn't exchange too many words with this one." He nodded toward Trent. "Liable to end up as libel."

"That's not bad," Trent said. "Although it would work better on the page. Can I borrow it?"

"Since when do you ask for permission to print something?"

"Never mind, I'll just use it as a direct quote."

"And you'll forget the quotation marks, or to credit who said it," the sheriff said.

"Anonymous source," Trent said.

"Without the—why am I...? Why are you still here, Trent? I already gave my office's official position."

"Yeah, but—"

The sheriff returned his attention to the woman. "And you are?"

The woman, still staring at Trent, shook her head as if clearing it, then said to Vance, "Dr. Brandy Phillips. Chief primatologist with the San Diego Zoo. I am also a medical doctor and psychologist."

"Don't forget nuclear physicist," Trent said.

Brandy glared at the reporter.

"Like Christmas Jones in James Bond," Deputy Dibble said.

"Just like that," Trent said.

"Why are you still here?" Sheriff Vance said to Trent.

"Because I—" Trent's response was cut off as Mable Hendricks began tugging on the sheriff's sleeve like a toddler needing to go potty.

Without looking down at Mable, the sheriff said, "Bathroom's still down the hall, Mable."

"No. No, Sheriff Vance," Mable said. "I need to tell you the Bigfoot expert is here. He can't get in because they still haven't made the steps handicap accessible, which I know I have been pushing for for the past ten—"

"Handicap?"

"He's in a wheelchair, sir."

"How the hell is he supposed to hike into the woods in a damn wheelchair?"

"He's got someone pushing him."

"Pushing him?" the sheriff said.

"Maybe he's a real good pusher," Deputy Dibble said.

"What a shitshow," the sheriff said as he and Deputy Dibble headed out the front door.

———————————

Brandy turned to Trent. She said under her breath, "Why didn't you tell me you were a reporter last night at the bar?"

"Would you have still had a drink with me?"

"No, of course not."

"Well, there's your answer."

"That's unethical."

"It's good reporting."

"But I was drunk."

"Very," Trent scoffed. "Would you like to report on the headache you most likely woke up with?"

"Well, it was all off the record. Isn't there a rule about not printing things off the record?"

"More of a guideline, really, and you need to tell me before you start blabbing."

"Sleazy."

"I prefer the term roguish, but yeah, okay, sleazy it is."

Brandy scowled, about to retort, but all that came out was a high-pitched snort.

Trent smirked. "Look, do you really think I'm looking to print a story about how you're jealous of your older sister, or that your little brother still wets his bed?"

"I told you that?"

"Don't worry, you didn't break anything scandalous. Other than the baboons at your zoo are assholes."

"Which they are," Brandy said.

"I didn't tell you I was a reporter because, at that moment, I wasn't a reporter. I enjoyed having a drink with you." He looked up at the ceiling as if calculating a math problem. "Several drinks with you."

"You told me you were a teacher."

"All right, that was a lie. I did once teach journalism at the local college…man, those kids were dumb."

"You're a liar."

"No, those kids were really dumb. One of them tried—"

"No, you're a liar in general."

"You may be right about that. But I'm searching for the truth. Look, I know you think this Bigfoot expedition is ridiculously stupid and a waste of time, and you're only here because your boss is making you—"

"How do you know th—?"

Trent tipped his thumb to his lips with his pinky in the air.

Brandy averted her eyes and said, "Never mind."

"But I think there *is* something out in those woods," Trent said.

"As a primatologist, please allow me to disagree with you. The notion of a Bigfoot is ridiculous."

"I agree, but, as you know, there are other primates in this world."

"You think it could be an actual ape? Like an escaped gorilla or baboon?" Brandy balled her fists.

"Ew, those damn baboons."

"No, nothing like that," Trent said.

"Then what? If you say a yeti or something, I will punch you in the face."

"Human," Trent said.

"Human? That's ridicu—"

Trent looked over Brandy's shoulder at the bustling outside the open front door. He said, "We should really get out there and meet this Bigfoot expert."

Brandy said, "No, you need to tell me this theory about this being a human."

"In time."

"In time?"

"I'm still theorizing," Trent said, starting for the door. "C'mon, let's find the sheriff."

Brandy stopped him, saying, "Is it me, or does the sheriff look like Denzel Washington?"

"It's not you," Trent said. "He's definitely the one that looks like Denzel." Trent continued toward the front door.

"Yeah, and—huh? Wait."

"C'mon," Trent said, gesturing to her to follow him.

———

"Ms. Phillips," the sheriff called as soon as Brandy and Trent stepped out of the building. He motioned her over with a wave of his arm, saying, "If you please, I'd like you to meet someone."

"Denzel beckons," Trent said under his breath.

"And you know what to do when Denzel beckons?" Brandy said.

"Go to Denzel?"

"Correct."

Trent shrugged. "He did say please."

A man in a wheelchair sat beside Sheriff Vance. The man's eyes seemed extra focused, but it was hard to tell if it was due to his intensity or the thick lenses of his glasses. He scrutinized Brandy as if determining if she bears false credentials.

"Ms. Phillips," the sheriff said, "This here is Hal Burke. He's a…well, he's a—"

"A fellow scientist, Miss Phillips," Burke said.

"I think it's pronounced *Doctor* Phillips," Trent said. "And what is it *you're* a doctor of, Mr. Burke?"

"And you are…?" Burke said to Trent.

"Leaving," Sheriff Vance said. "What are you even still doing here, Trent?"

"My job," Trent said.

"Which is?"

"Exposing stupidity?"

Burke gestured behind him with his thumb, saying, "Apparently that's his job."

Everyone suddenly noticed the young man standing behind Burke's wheelchair. Everyone stared silently at him.

The young man said, "What?"

"And you are?" Trent asked the young man.

"The token Asian, apparently," the young man said,

pushing his glasses more securely onto his face and looking around at the others. "And I'm beginning to worry that I'm wearing a red shirt."

Burke said, "I told you, we are dealing with sasquatch, not bulls."

"No, because of *Star Tr*—never mind."

"What's your name?" Trent said.

"Norm Yoo."

Deputy Dibble said, "I think my cousin went to Norm U. Like, online courses or something, right?"

"Can we please just carry on like before, like I'm not here?" Norm said.

"We should be going," Burke said. "Squatch move fast. This one could be out of the state before we know it."

Trent turned to Brandy and said, "Is that true, *Dr. Phillips*? Sasquatch move fast?"

Brandy said, "How would I know?"

"You are the trained primatologist with several degrees in the field, are you not?" Trent said. "What are your thoughts about the migratory habits of sasquatch?"

"I don't—"

Trent said, "Sorry, what are your thoughts about sasquatch in general?"

"That they don't exist?" Brandy said.

"Now, look here," Burke said, "Mock all you want, but perhaps you want to tell me my paraplegia doesn't exist either. The paraplegia caused by the very real and painful broken back from a very real sasquatch. Perhaps you want—"

A cacophonous trumpet car horn split the air, causing everyone to jump.

Sheriff Vance lowered his hat on his brow and said, "What the fuck now?"

An emerald green 1950s model Land Rover pulled up in front of the sheriff's office, and after another shrill blast of the horn, a man stepped out of the vehicle's right-side driver's seat.

Deputy Dibble said, "He drove that car backwards like he was in England."

The man—in his mid-fifties with ruddy skin and twinkling eyes—wore what could easily have been mistaken for a safari Halloween costume: beige shorts, button-down shirt, knee-high socks. He ceremoniously doffed his leather Side Snap hat and said in a heavy British accent, "Major Nigel Niven at your service." He returned the hat to his head and smoothed his thick mustache. "Now, what have we here?"

The sheriff stepped up, offering his hand. "Sheriff Malcolm Vance."

The Major took his hand and said, "You, lad, remind me of a tracker I knew in Kruger. You of course are too young, and have not the accent, but a relative perhaps? Father?"

Sheriff Vance smiled with his Denzel teeth. But his eyes did not match the gesture. "No, I don't believe so. My family has been in America since its beginnings. But I am happy to be of service to you, if I knew what it is you've come for."

"My dear boy, I am here on behalf of the honorable Senator Jenaway, a hunting buddy of mine. Did he not inform you of my impending arrival?"

Sheriff Vance tipped his hip, resting one hand on his gun belt and the other on the butt of his revolver. He smiled with only his mouth again and said, "Well, Major, it's been a while since I've been called *boy*, dear or otherwise, and I'd prefer to leave it that way. As for the senator, he has not been fully clear as to whom he'd be sending for this expedition. I'm afraid I have been left a little out of the loop."

"As have I," Brandy said, eyeing the Major with thinly veiled disgust.

The Major eyed Brandy back, but disgust was not the emotion in his eyes. "Well, hello, my dear. And you are?"

"Dr. Brandy Philips," Brandy said. "Chief Primatologist for The San Diego Zoo."

"Splendid," said the Major, taking her hand and kissing it ceremoniously.

Brandy yanked her hand back as if from a snapping crocodile.

"And I'm Hal Burke," Burke said, waving from his wheelchair. "Major?"

The Major continued gazing at Brandy, saying, "Primatologist? Splendid. I have an amazing silverback gorilla specimen in my home in Tuscany." He smoothed his mustache. "Perhaps you would like to see it some time?"

Brandy coughed into her hand and said, "Sorry, I think I just threw up a little."

"I'll take that as a maybe," said the Major. "Splendid."

Burke waved his hand, saying, "Major? Major, I am Hal Burke. Major?" Burke then said over his shoulder to Norm, "Probably doesn't hear me."

"I think he hears you," Norm said.

The Major said to Brandy, "You know, I once met Diane Fossey."

"Hopefully not at the end," Trent said.

"No, no, of course not, although…" the Major said, and then looked off wistfully.

"I wouldn't finish that sentence," Trent said.

"We should probably be heading into the office to get a game plan," the sheriff said. He walked toward the front door, shaking his head. Deputy Dibble followed closely, like a birding dog.

Trent said to Major Niven, "Does the sheriff really look like a tracker at Kruger?"

"My boy, that one looks just like Denzel Washington," the Major said and then followed the sheriff.

Trent turned to Brandy. "See? Everyone says it."

"I see that."

"I bet you'd be up for a stuffed specimen at Denzel's Tuscany home."

"As long as it wasn't a dead animal."

Trent paused for a moment, and then said, "That was pretty good."

"I thought so too."

They followed the Major into the office.

Burke and Norm remained behind, regarding the steps leading into the office.

"Um, Sheriff?" Burke called.

Chapter 3

An hour later it was 10:00am, and the same group of people stood in front of the sheriff's office again. This time they carried large backpacks—Norm carrying both his and Burke's pack. Trent—with no pack—trotted up to Brandy.

Trent said, "Good, I didn't miss you guys."

"Where were you?" Brandy said.

"I had a few phone calls to make."

"Wife?" Brandy said, as if confirming an obvious detail.

"No. Research," Trent said.

"Research on your wife?"

"Huh? What are you—I'm not married. Why would you—?"

"Sorry," Brandy said in a manner of habitual penitence. "It's just…you threw me for a loop, being so charming and all last night, and now…it feels like some kind of scam."

"I wasn't scamming you. I promise. I really enjoyed hanging out with you last night," Trent said.

"Okay. Well we're just about to head out here, so you're just in time."

"What's the plan?

"We're going to head to the campsite where the attack occurred."

"And Major Monkey Murderer is going to track the beast from there?"

"Something like that," Brandy grumbled. "Hey, where's your gear?"

"Gear?"

Raising his voice, Sheriff Vance announced, "We can access most of the trails into the deeper woods right here. It's not too far to the campsite."

Major Niven unslung the Springfield 03 from his shoulder and held it before him as if about to charge San Juan Hill. "I shall go ahead, alone. I shan't be slackened by the inexpert. A tracker must be free to track at a brisk pace."

"I prefer we all stick together," Sheriff Vance said.

"My dear b—sir, I must heartily disagree with you. As the game expert, I must be allowed to adequately hunt the objective prey."

"Prey?" Brandy said. "I thought we were trying to observe and study?"

Major Niven arched an eyebrow in her direction. "I know many who have observed and studied a lion the moment before it tore the jugular from their throats."

"We go together," the sheriff said. "I don't want you out of communication with the group, and mistaking us, or anyone else, for game. I am in charge here, and that's final."

"But—"

"Final," the sheriff said.

"Of course, Mr. Model Modern Major-Sheriff," the Major said. With a sarcastic flourish, he snapped off a salute while bringing his rifle down into an Order Arms position. As the butt of the gun struck the ground at his feet, there was a deafening discharge. The Major's hat lifted from his head on a geyser of red like a child's lawn game. The hat then landed back onto his head as it was before, if not a little crooked. The Major's eyes seemed to focus on the people gathered around him, as if inquiring as to the source of the report. Then his eyes crossed and he dropped to the ground in a heap.

A girl began to scream—scratch that, Burke began screaming, high pitched and frantic like a woman in a B movie.

Sheriff Vance paused a moment, regarding the heap, and said, "Aw, goddamn it."

Burke continued his shrieking.

Vance turned to Norm and, gesturing toward Burke, said, "Can you calm him down or something?"

"Me?" Norm said, blinking.

"Yeah, you," the sheriff said.

Norm tapped Burke's shoulder with the tips of his fingers, saying, "Now, now…there, there?"

"How very maternal," Brandy grumbled toward Norm. She then crouched beside Burke and embraced him, as a mother would to comfort a child. Burke nuzzled his face into her bosom, his hand creeping down along the arch of her back, toward her ass. Brandy pushed him away and stood. She looked at Norm and said, "You were doing fine."

Norm tapped Burke's shoulder again, saying, "There, there?"

"This is going to be a lot of paperwork," Vance said.

"Sheriff, a man is dead," Brandy said.

"Which is going to require a lot of paperwork. I have to call in the coroner, state forensics, next of kin… god knows what else."

"The coroner sounds about right," Norm said.

"Deputy Dibble?" Vance said.

"Yes, Sheriff?" Dibble said, snapping off a salute.

"Take them to the campsite," the sheriff said. "We can at least get that out of the way."

"We're still going forward with this?" Brandy said.

"Look," the sheriff said, "you all are here, the senator wants this done. I'm not going through the hassle of gathering like this again. We move forward."

"But a man is dead," Brandy said.

"And that is unfortunate," the sheriff said. "But there are a bunch of kids dead, too, and our job is to find out why. We do the job."

"Isn't it bad luck to already have someone die before we even get started?" Trent said.

"Why are you still here, Trent?" the sheriff said.

"Obviously, it's to logically point out things that are illogical," Trent said.

"I thought that's his job," the sheriff said, pointing at Norm.

"Huh?" Norm said. "Sorry, I'm a little focused on how exactly I get this fleck of brain off my glasses."

"Just use your shirt and wipe it off," the sheriff said.

"I don't think I want to do that."

"Look," the sheriff said, turning back to Trent, "That guy was an idiot." He pointed at the heap of Major at his feet. "He was clearly reckless, and probably drunk. It would have been bad luck for him to still be going in there with you. Take this as a sign of *good* luck."

"You said you," Trent said.

"Huh?"

"You said going in there with *you*, not *us*."

"Yeah, because now I have goddamn paperwork."

"Then who is going to lead while we're out there?"

"Deputy Dibble is capable."

"Yup," said Dibble.

"Seriously?" Trent said.

The sheriff chewed his lip and regarded the deputy a moment. "Yup," he said finally.

"Shouldn't we have someone with experience dealing with big animals?" Trent said.

The sheriff gestured to Brandy. "You got someone who deals with gorillas here." He then gestured to Burke. "And whatever this guy deals with."

"A Bigfoot?" Trent said. "What killed those kids is clearly a bear."

"No," Burke wailed through his snot and tears, "it was a squatch."

"Jesus," Trent said.

"For once we agree, Trent," the sheriff said.

"About the bear?"

"No. Jesus, that guy needs a freaking tissue."

"If you got them, I could use one too," Norm said, waving his glasses, trying to get a dangling glob of red off the lens.

"Look," the sheriff said, "Dibble, take them into the campsite. I'll have Quint meet you on the way?"

"Quint," Dibble said to himself with reverence.

"You mean Quint, Quint? Like, *the* Quint?" Trent said, barking an incredulous laugh. "Didn't you say drunk and reckless was a bad thing?"

"No one knows those woods better," the sheriff said. "We get Quint."

With a final flick of his wrist, Norm got the brain off his glasses; it flung up and landed in his hair. "Um, excuse me? We're seriously getting some old grizzled guy named Quint to hunt this thing?"

"How do you know he's old and grizzled?" the sheriff said.

"Is he?" Norm said.

"Yeah, so?"

"You know—the guy—the name…*Quint*?" Norm said. "We need a bigger boat?"

The sheriff shook his head. "Bigger boat? What the hell is he talking about? And this kid is supposed to be the logical one?"

"You seriously don't see this?" Norm said.

They stared at him, silently shaking their heads.

The kid shrugged. "All right."

"Get going," the sheriff said, "daylight is wasting."

Brandy gestured to the corpse on the ground. "Shouldn't we say something?"

"Yeah," the sheriff said, "this sucks."

———

"Are you going to be okay?" Trent asked Brandy as they headed into the woods. The bottoms of her eyelids quivered with tiny pools of tears.

"I can't get the look of the Major's face out of my mind," she said. "I've seen plenty of apes in their last moments, often cradled in my own arms, and believe me, they can be so human it's spooky, but never…I've never seen a person killed like that."

"I have," Trent said, his voice dropping to almost a whisper, as if the answer was for his ears only. He then said, "And it's true what they say, you get used to it if it happens enough."

Brandy snapped her head toward him and watched the many emotions fight for his face. "Sounds like you have a story," she said.

"Several. But none I'm ready to tell," Trent said. "I wasn't always a small town beat writer. Back in the day, I'd seen a lot of…things. And you start to just get used to the death. But what you don't get used to is the act of killing. That inner impetus for humans to keep taking what others can't afford to give."

A squawk came from far behind them. It was Burke saying, "Damn it, Norm, we're falling behind, catch up."

Brandy and Trent looked over their shoulders to see Norm muscling Burke's wheelchair over divots.

"Burke seems to have gotten over it pretty fast," Trent said.

"Well, I suppose a healthy handful of my ass will do that for someone."

Trent raised his eyebrows. "Yeah? Seriously? He cop a feel when you comforted him?"

"Something like that."

"Wow, what an asshole."

Brandy looked over her shoulder and regarded Burke berating Norm in the distance. "Do you think he was always like that? Or do you think he's like that now because of the wheelchair?"

"You think the wheelchair is, like, possessed or something?" Trent said.

"Huh?"

"An evil wheelchair?"

"No. Huh?" Brandy said. "I meant, is being in a wheelchair bringing out his anger?"

Trent smiled. "I know what you meant. I was joking." He looked over his shoulder at Burke. "I think he's always been like that. Everyone is an asshole deep down, it's just how much can be suppressed."

"Oh, god, you're not one of those cynics are you?"

"Afraid so."

"I'm going to bring you to meet the chimpanzees at the zoo. Lock you in the room with them."

"That will make me less cynical, huh?"

"No, I want to watch them throw poop at you."

"Deal."

Neither talked for several steps, then Brandy said, "So, what is your theory about this sasquatch being human?"

Trent said, "I'm still formulating that theory—hold on…do you hear that?"

"I hear Burke bitching at Norm."

"No…I hear…singing."

Ahead of them, a voice sang: "*Farewell and adieu, you fair Spanish ladies, farewell and adieu, you ladies of Spain….*"

"Hey, that's Quint," Deputy Dibble said.

"Goddamn it," Norm called.

They turned back toward Norm, who had stopped pushing Burke and now stood with his hands on his hips.

"Everything all right?" Trent called.

"He's even singing the damn song," Norm said, throwing his arms in the air. "You seriously don't see this?"

"Song? What about it?" Trent said.

"You've seriously never heard this song anywhere?"

"I think it was in Moby Dick," Brandy said.

"Jesus Christ," Norm said with his hands back on his hips.

"C'mon," Burke barked. "We still have to get over those roots there."

"We?" Norm said.

"Yeah, I'll help as much as I can," Burke said, his hands staying in his lap.

Norm groaned and began muscling the chair forward again.

The group approached a figure leaning against a tree. He wore dark gray khaki pants that may have once been beige, a thick flannel jacket, and a baseball cap pulled over his eyes. The cap was so worn the original message was all but forgotten, but a few letters remained: an O, an R, a C, and an A (these letters bringing another groan from Norm). The man's stubble-strewn face was so weathered it was hard to tell if the hue of his skin was from the sun, genetics, or filth.

"This is Quint," Deputy Dibble said in a tone reminiscent of a dog's wagging tail.

The man leaning against the tree said, "Name's Raoul Leonard; my friends call me Quint."

"Why do they call you Quint?" Brandy said.

"I was the seventh son of a seventh son."

"Isn't quint five?" Norm said.

"Shh," Brandy said.

"Light is waning, time to move," Quint said. "Nighttime is not the right time in these here woods." He hefted an enormous double barrel shotgun from beside the tree.

"Does Elmer Fudd know you have his gun?" Norm said.

Quint eyed Norm and said, "Just a warning: wiseasses are like catnip to bears."

"Do bears *like* catnip?" Norm said.

Quint turned and began walking into the woods, singing, "*Farewell and adieu….*"

No one in the group moved.

Deputy Dibble took off his hat and ran his hand over his head, saying, "I think we are, like, supposed to follow him?"

The others fell in behind Quint. Norm watched them go. Burke began squawking. "Let's go. Yoo, Yoo…."

"No, you, you…" Norm mocked and began pushing the wheelchair.

By the time they reached the campsite—now deemed a crime scene—the sun, a peepshow of flickering starbursts through the canopy of trees, was beginning to edge west. The only sounds were from the broken police tape slithering across the ground in the barely perceptible breeze and Quint chomping on sunflower seeds and spitting them over his shoulder. Paint was sprayed on the ground to mark the outlines of the bodies that had been strewn about that fateful night. Brandy looked down to see the headless outline of J.J.'s corpse. She then followed his head's path to Debbie's corpse, the outline of J.J.'s head nestled against the outline of Debbie's bosom.

"CSI: Sleepy Hollow?" Trent said.

"You're more familiar with the police report than I am," Brandy said, "but were any of the victims eaten?"

"Not a single bite mark."

"I'm no bear expert, but does that gel with a bear attack?"

"Why don't you ask the bear expert?" Trent said, nodding toward Quint, who was leaning against a tree drinking from a silver flask.

"I think the only animals that guy is an expert on right now are pink elephants."

"Does this look more like an attack from a primate?" Trent asked.

"Perhaps. One in the grips of rage, maybe. No tool marks on this decapitation?"

"No. Police think it was knocked from his torso. His facial bone structure looked like a 1000 piece jigsaw puzzle."

"That doesn't bode well for your human attacker theory."

"I suppose not."

"I hate to say it, but…" she let her statement trail off.

"What?" Trent said.

Brandy looked over at Burke, who was squawking something at Norm over his shoulder.

"Bigfoot?" Trent said to Brandy.

"No," Brandy said with a reluctant sigh. "There has to be a logical explanation."

"I agree," Trent said. He glanced over at Quint.

Quint took another swig from his flask as Deputy

Dibble moseyed up to him.

"So what do you think, Mr. Quint?" Dibble said.

Quint spit out several seeds and shrugged, saying, "Bear's in the woods…people's in the woods…" He smiled sheepishly. *"Farewell and adieu, you fine Spanish ladies…."*

Norm darted his head to see the expressions of the others, searching for any recognition, but then shook his head in defeat.

"So you think it *is* a bear?" Trent said to Quint.

"Nothing else I know that can cause this here damage," Quint said, nodding toward the outlines of carnage. He then took a sip from his flask.

Deputy Dibble inspected Quint's face. "How do you drink and chew on them seeds at the same time?"

Burke said, "I know of something else that can cause this kind of damage. And I think it's about time you all gave me the respect I've earned, as a casualty of the Squatch Wars, to listen to my theories."

Trent and Brandy simultaneously said, "The Squatch Wars?"

"Here we go," Norm said.

Burke said, "The battle between an ancient race of giants and humans for these sacred woods."

"You call it the Squatch Wars?" Trent said.

"I think it sounds about right," Burke said.

"It sounds awesome," Deputy Dibble said. He then said, in a voice not unlike a Monster Truck commercial, "Squatch Wars."

"It sounds ridiculous," Trent said.

"Here we go," Norm repeated.

Burke sneered at Trent, "If you want to mock me for my life's journey, then why don't *you* try sitting in this here wheelchair and let *him…*" he jammed his thumb over his shoulder toward Norm, "push *you* around for a while? And I'll go traipsing through the woods without a care."

"*Can* we try that for a while?" Norm said.

"You don't need that chair?" Deputy Dibble said. "That's weird you'd be sitting in it this whole time."

"That's your life journey?" Trent said.

"I believe we've already established that, *Trent*." Burke said the journalist's name as if it were a mouthful of shit. "I'm the only one who knows the intricacies of the squatch."

"Because it was a squatch that put you in that chair?" Trent said.

"Yes, *Trent*. Do *you* know that a squatch's skin is not unlike a shark's skin under all that hair, rough and so tightly packed with cells it can repel lower caliber bullets?"

"They're bulletproof?" Trent said with a grin.

"Yes, *Trent*. Do you know that they always move clockwise from a set location for about a month at a time, moving on with the phases of the moon?"

"Do they move counterclockwise in Australia?" Norm said.

"Hey, like the Coriolis Effect," Deputy Dibble said.

Brandy snapped her head toward the deputy, raising her eyebrows.

"What?" the deputy said. "It's a thing…I think."

Trent said, "If there is a race of these animals, then why have no remains ever been found?" He gestured around at the forest. "You'd think some evidence would be found."

Burke said, "The molecular structure of their skin, muscles, and bones are designed to accelerate the breakdown of decomposition. A thousand pound squatch can literally decompose in a matter of minutes."

"Convenient," Trent said.

"And impossible," Brandy said.

"Oh, let's hear from the expert, please, Miss Phillips," Burke said.

"It's Doctor," Brandy said.

"And you are a doctor of Squatchology?" Burke sneered.

"Squatchology?" Trent said. "Did you just come up with that too?"

"Unfortunately, no," Norm said.

"I gave up my ability to walk to pursue the study of these animals," Burke sneered. "I faced one of these beasts down in the heat of a stifling forest, and its roar still tattoos my heart to this day, the fury of its red eyes still haunting my dreams."

"They have red eyes?" Deputy Dibble said. "That's awesome."

Burke continued. "I know its movements because I have been stalked. I know the feel of its skin because my fists have landed upon its flesh with futile blows as it took me in its massive hands and severed my spine. I know its physiology because I have since sought out every expert to learn about every aspect of these beasts, so I can better understand what happened to me when my ability to walk was snatched from me."

Burke's words were followed by stunned silence, until Trent said, "Vespa."

"What's that, *Trent*?" Burke said.

"It was a Vespa," Trent said.

"What are you talking about?" Brandy said.

"It was a Vespa that took his ability to walk," Trent said.

"The Bigfoot's name was Vespa?" Deputy Dibble said.

"No," Trent said. "Burke here lost the use of his legs in a scooter accident. That's what I was doing while you all were planning this little expedition earlier at the police station. I was on the phone with the research department of my paper, and they told me Burke here was paralyzed when he was clipped by a Vespa while jaywalking at San Bernardino Community College in 1998."

In a voice not unlike a Monster Truck commercial, Norm said, "Vespa Wars."

"Did you know about this?" Brandy asked Norm.

"What? Are you kidding?" Norm said. "You think I'd have left that fact alone?"

"Fact is," Trent said, "there never was any squatch attack, or Squatch Wars for that matter. Burke here is a liar."

"That would have been really helpful information before I pushed him all the way out here," Norm said.

"That's not true," Burke whined. "I did see a squatch. I did confront one. It did attack me."

"Before or after you were run down by a Vespa?" Trent said.

Burke lowered his head and said, "Before." He raised his head again and glanced at his companions. "When I was a boy, I'd hear rustling and strange grunts from the deep woods behind my home. And I knew—"

Quint flicked up his massive shotgun, and a deafening thunderclap rang through the forest.

With shoulders scrunched and hands over their ears, the group turned to find his target.

Two young women and a young man stood frozen at the tree line. Their eyes were wide, mouths dropped open, and a flurry of leaves sprinkled down and around them.

Chapter 4

Quint spat out his seeds and took a swig from his flask.

"What the hell are you doing?" Trent shouted.

"Heard something," Quint said.

"I don't think I'll ever hear anything again," Norm said, jiggling his pinky in his ear.

"You hear something, and you just shoot at it?" Trent shouted.

"If I'd shot at it, they'd be dead," Quint said, gesturing with his flask toward the three newly arrived hikers.

"You're crazy," Trent said to Quint. He then turned and walked toward the three people who'd just arrived.

Brandy and Deputy Dibbles followed him.

Quint shrugged. He glanced over at Norm, who was still jiggling at his ear and making cascading humming sounds as if practicing scales.

"Your hearing will be back in a minute," Quint told him.

"Hmmm…Ahhh…it's more a ringing than hearing loss," Norm said.

"That will go away."

Norm stopped jiggling and looked for a moment at the grizzled hunter. "Why do they call you Quint?" Norm said.

Quint eyed him and spat out his seeds. "I'm a Piquet aficionado."

"That doesn't mean anything to me."

"Look it up on your Goggle, son."

"You mean Google?"

Quint smiled. "*Farewell and adieu, you fine Spanish ladies…*"

"You're a real fucker," Norm said.

Trent, Brandy, and Deputy Dibble gathered around the newly arrived hikers. The two young women were crying. The young man was regarding the leaves still fluttering above them.

"Are you all right?" Brandy said to them.

The young man, a wiry surfer dude type, said, "Whoa."

The two young women, a blonde and brunette, cried harder.

The brunette pointed at Quint and said, "That man is scary."

The blonde said, "That man is mean."

Deputy Dibble said, "As a duly elected law enforcement representative of the local municipality, I need to ask what you are doing at this crime scene?"

"Are deputies elected?" Trent said.

"Duly…appointed?" Deputy Dibble said.

"I think that's closer," Trent said.

"More like hired, I think?" Brandy said.

"That sounds right," Trent said.

"As a duly hired law enforcement representative of the local municipality, I need to ask what you are doing at this crime scene?" Deputy Dibble said.

"Whoa, crime scene. Crazy," the dude said. "Like, we didn't even think about that. We're from the local college."

"What college is that?" Brandy said.

"The local one," the dude said.

"Which one?" Brandy said.

"The one that's right close by," the dude said.

"Yeah, but—" Brandy said.

"There is a college close by," Deputy Dibble said.

"But which—?"

The dude said, "We, like, came from the local college way out here to…like, what was it?" he said to the girls.

"Build a memorial shrine," the brunette said, wiping away her tears.

"Deidre was my best friend," the blonde said, wiping her own tears.

"Debbie," the brunette said.

"Debbie was my best friend," the blonde said.

"When we heard about this tragedy, we knew we had to come out here and build a memorial shrine and take pictures of it and post it all over school to remind others about our friends," the brunette said.

"We are going to be models for their grief," the blonde said.

"That sounds very noble," Trent said, eyeing the dude. "Building a shrine like that?"

The dude raised his eyebrows and said, "I have the camera."

"Yeah? I bet," Trent said.

"And the car," the dude said.

"It's late to be hiking out here," Brandy said. "It will be dark soon."

The brunette said, "Well, he couldn't get the car until later, so we had to wait."

The blonde said, "So he suggested we camp out here in the middle of nowhere, spend the night, and then in the early morning we will have the perfect lighting for our pictures."

"That's a logical idea," Trent said to the dude.

"I thought so," the dude said.

"You were probably only able to procure a single tent though, huh?" Trent said to the dude.

"Yeah," the brunette said. "How did you know that?"

"It's small, but good enough to share," the blonde said.

"That's what she said," Brandy said.

"You beat me to it," Trent said to Brandy, and they both grinned.

"It is what I said," the blonde said.

"Sounds like you have it all figured out," Trent said to the dude.

"Didn't expect an old dude with a shotgun to shoot at us though," the dude said.

"I bet you didn't. Or that people would be here investigating the maulings that happened in this exact spot only a couple of days ago." Trent said.

"Whoa, yeah, I guess that's not what was on my mind," the dude said.

Deputy Dibble said, "As a duly elected law enforcement representative of the local municipality, I need to ask what you are doing at this crime scene?"

"Duly hired," Brandy said.

"Shoot, sorry," Deputy Dibble said. "But I do need to know why you are here."

"Um, we just told you that," the dude said.

"Yeah, but, *why* are you here?" Deputy Dibble said.

"We're making a memorial shrine," the brunette said.

"Yeah, but—" Deputy Dibble began.

"I think they're going to need to camp here with us tonight," Brandy said. "It's safer that way."

"The more the merrier for this guy, right?" Trent said, slapping the dude on the back.

"Heh," the dude made an awkward laugh. "Yeah…?"

Deputy Dibble said, "As a duly elected law enforcement representative of the local municipality, I ordain that you stay here tonight for safety." He looked at Brandy and Trent.

Trent shrugged and nodded. "Sounds about right."

"Hired," Brandy said.

———————

Trent walked up to Brandy.

"Where have you been?" she asked.

"Writing up some notes while everything is still fresh in my mind. And trying to find a cell signal."

"Anything?"

"Nope." Trent regarded the area. The crime scene had become a camping site again. Several tents were erected and campers mulled around a large fire. Quint stood looking into the flames, drinking from his flask. The dude and the two girls sat cross-legged, nervously regarding Quint. Deputy Dibble patrolled the camp like a blind guard dog. Burke and Norm were nowhere to be seen.

"Dibble find anything?" Trent asked.

"He warned us that he smelled a skunk, but I think it was the dude and the girls off smoking a joint."

Trent inspected the array of tents while rubbing his chin.

Brandy, watching him, said, "Not sure where you're sleeping, big boy?"

"Um…yeah. I guess I didn't think this through," Trent said.

"Didn't think that hiking miles into deep woods would require some kind of gear when it got dark?"

"Guess I didn't think I'd get this far."

"Chasing the story?"

Trent looked at her and grinned. "Chasing something," he said. His eyes lingered on her.

She smiled, her eyes lingering on him. Then she

looked toward the fire and said, "Quint doesn't have a tent either. You can snuggle up to the fire with him. Maybe he'll even share his blanket."

"I could always see if they'll let me into their tent," Trent said, pointing to the dude and the two girls.

"I bet you'd like that," Brandy said.

"They're such great conversationalists."

"I'm sure conversation is why the dude came out here."

"Where are Burke and Norm?" Trent said. "Should we be worried at all?"

"They went to set camera traps. And, yes, we should be worried."

"Camera traps? Is it camera season already?"

Brandy chuckled and said, "No, donkey, camera traps are motion-detecting cameras. They're hoping to find evidence of a Bigfoot."

"And why didn't you bring any such technical equipment?"

"Who says I didn't?"

"But you aren't setting it up?"

"There's no Bigfoot to catch."

"But there's something."

"And you think it's human," Brandy said. "Are you ever going to fill me in on that theory?"

"I'm getting to it. It might cost you your tent."

"You're sounding like that dude now," Brandy said, nodding toward the college students.

Deputy Dibble's voice rang out, "Halt, who goes there?" He had one hand on the butt of his firearm and the other hand extended forward.

Out of the woods came the familiar sight of a man pushing another in a wheelchair.

"Looks like Burke and Norm are back, let's see what they have to report," Trent said, heading toward the fire.

"Whatever it is, I'm sure it will be totally scientifically accurate," Brandy said, following him.

With the entire expedition—including its recently arrived stowaways—gathered around the fire, Burke announced, "I have taken liberty to employ some rather high-tech scientific equipment."

"We swung by RadioShack earlier today," Norm said.

Quint, who was standing beside Norm, chuckled.

"You've heard of RadioShack?" Norm said to the hunter.

"Yeah," Quint said, eyeing him, "it's what I call my outhouse."

"Please don't tell me why," Norm said.

"Anyway," Burke said, glaring at Brandy, "at least one of us will do some actual scientific investigating. My cameras will be able to spot anything coming our way."

Brandy said, "Does that include Vespas?"

"Whoa," the rest of the group groaned in distaste.

"Harsh," Trent said, scrunching his face.

"What?" Brandy said. "Too soon? It was like ten years ago."

"Even I wouldn't have said that one," Norm said.

The dude began chuckling with his half-closed eyes and said, "Ha, Vespa."

"You can attack me personally all you want," Burke said, "but my science will speak for itself."

"What science?" Brandy said. "What science could possibly explain rapidly dissolving Bigfoot corpses?"

"Well we haven't been able to study that aspect because the corpses dissolve," Burke said.

"How expedient," Brandy said. "One can't prove a negative, so the bodies miraculously disappear in your world. It's ridiculous and not even remotely based on any kind of scientific principle. If you can provide any possible science-based explanation for it, maybe I'll listen."

There was silence. Then Norm spoke up timidly. "Well, it's possible there is some sort of hydrochloric compound embedded in their tissue and a base element present in their bloodstream counteracting the compound. Perhaps when they die, which stops the circulation of the base element in the blood, the hydrochloric compound is triggered to dissolve the flesh in which it is embedded?"

Everyone stared at Norm.

"What?" Norm said. "I'm a biochemistry major at Cal Tech."

"What are you doing working for this guy?" Trent said, gesturing toward Burke.

"I needed an internship," Norm said. "Turned out to be a Kramerica situation."

"Kramerica?" Trent said.

"You know, *Seinfeld*," Norm said.

The dude burst into laughter and said, "Hydrochloric."

"That wasn't helpful, Norm," Brandy said.

Norm shrugged. "Sorry."

Deputy Dibble took off his hat and rubbed his hand over his head, saying, "Looky, here, we need to start choosing who's going to be taking shifts for watch. I'll take first watch. Who's next?"

"It's getting really late," Burke said, stretching his arms, "and I am wiped from the journey; I think I need to be getting to my tent."

"I'll get you there immediately," Norm said, pushing Burke's wheelchair.

The dude stood and stretched, saying to the girls, "I got some wine coolers in the tent, c'mon."

Brandy began edging toward her tent. Trent grabbed at her arm, but she slapped his hand away.

Deputy Dibble put his fists on his hips and puffed out his chest, saying, "Looks like we got me, Quint, and Mr. Tann—"

Before Dibble could finish, Brandy grabbed Trent by his arm and pulled him toward her tent.

"So it's just me and you, Quint," the deputy said, but when he turned, Quint was nowhere to be found.

Brandy's tent was cramped, but warm. She said to Trent, "We sleep back-to-back, and you're on your own as far as the sleeping bag goes. If you try to climb in it with me, I get Quint's shotgun, got it?"

"Yikes. Sure," Trent said. "Want a drink?"

"Huh?"

He held up two wine coolers. "I may have borrowed a couple of these from the dude."

"You stole their wine coolers? You really are sleazy."

"Roguish," he said. "But I can return them if you'd prefer."

"Give me that," she said, snatching the bottle. "I didn't even realize they still sold these things. What is this 1988?"

"Careful drinking these; they still pack a punch. I don't want to hear about any more familial bedwetting," Trent said.

"Ha-ha, very funny," she scolded. "You got an opener for this?"

"Opener? They're wine coolers. Aren't all wine coolers twist off?"

"Not these apparently."

"You're the scientist, didn't you bring some kind of gear?"

"Not for wine coolers," Brandy said. She brought the bottle to her mouth and opened the top with her teeth.

"Jesus, don't ruin those perfect teeth," Trent said.

"Desperate times, desperate measures."

Trent stared at the top of his unopened bottle.

"Give me that," Brandy said, snatching it from him.

"Wouldn't want you to ruin that roguish smile." She opened it with her teeth and handed it back to him.

"Will you marry me?" Trent said.

"Depends on how good this theory about a human Bigfoot is. Now spill it."

"Very well," Trent said. "But again, I'm still formulating it."

"I don't care. Spill it."

"Okay," Trent said. "You're maybe too young to remember the short-lived Mega Wrestling Stars League of the late 80s?"

"I remember the MWSL," Brandy said. "My brother loved it. It's what got him into wrestling."

"You didn't mention the bed wetter was a wrestler."

"Different brother," Brandy said. "My big brother. Scholarship to Ohio State, alternate on the Olympic team. And when I say big brother, I mean he is big. I must have failed to mention him before."

"Maybe I should stop being a sleaze?"

"I don't think you can," Brandy said and smiled. "But, yes, I know the wrestling league."

"All right," Trent said, returning her smile. "So you probably remember the league's biggest star, Rad Rocky Hollywood?"

"Of course. The guy with the long blond mullet, right? Didn't he get kicked out of the league for breaking a ref's leg?" Brandy said. "He had some kind of rage syndrome or something?"

"And what causes rage syndrome in some athletes?"

"Could be related to concussions. We in the medical field are starting to understand the effects of head injuries on people's personalities."

"I'm sure you could identify other things that cause rage syndrome?"

"Of course."

"Like steroids?"

"A lot of them, yes."

"Rad Rocky Hollywood didn't leave wrestling because he was kicked out," Trent said. "Rumor has it, he walked away from it and then disappeared, went off grid and became a survivalist. The rumors said he was taking serious hardcore roids, like shit they give racehorses. He was getting too big and too mean. He couldn't control his rage any longer and he was becoming just too damn strong. Some say he had even tacked on nearly a foot in height."

"That's impossible," Brandy said.

"I'm just telling it how I heard it." Trent shrugged. "Another side effect of the drugs was hair. Lots of hair growing all over his body. Like that Wolfman disease."

"Hypertrichosis?" Brandy said. "Again, that's ridiculous. That's genetic, you don't get that from steroids."

"I didn't say it was Hyper-whatever, I said it was like it. It was—" He cocked his head. "Did you hear that?"

"What?" Brandy said.

"I don't know," Trent said, cocking his head again. "Probably Deputy Dibble doing something…"

"Dibble-like?" Trent said.

"Exactly," Brandy said. "Okay, so we have a taller, hairier Rad Rocky, I'm still not following your point?"

"Really? I thought you were smar—" Trent cocked his head again. "You seriously don't hear that?"

"No. And what am I supposed to be seeing?"

"Hearing."

"No, your point. What am I supposed to be seeing about your point?"

"That kid who survived the attack here the other night—name was Davis Dugger—he said that before the thing—the Bigfoot—jumped from the tree, it slapped its chest twice and raised its hands to its ears, which is…" Trent rotated his hand on his wrist and extended it toward her, encouraging her to finish his thought.

Brandy watched his hand and shrugged. "What?"

"Slapping one's chest and raising one's hands to one's ears is…"

Brandy shook her head, saying, "Not something Bigfoots do? I don't know."

"It's Rad Rocky's signature calling card. He always did that before going off the top rope."

"Oh yeah," Brandy said, looking toward the back of the tent. "I forgot about that."

Trent didn't say anything. His head was cocked as if listening still.

"You okay?" Brandy said.

"Yeah. Sorry."

"So you're saying the Bigfoot slapped its chest so that makes it human? Several primates slap their chests in that manner."

"Including humans. And one particular human that we know of."

"Yeah, but—"

"And every injury inflicted on a victim that night is consistent with one of Rad Rocky's moves. Elbow from the top rope, as he'd done on the tent. Forearm shiver, as he applied to one male, killing him. Palm plant to another, putting a male in a coma. Clothes-line, decapitating the senator's son. And a body slam, paralyzing our key witness."

"That could all be coincidence, most likely they are injuries also consistent with bear attacks. There is no way a human would attack a campsite like that. Humans don't—"

Her statement was cut off by roaring—a sound very much like a human trying to sound like an animal. This was followed by girls—and possibly Burke—screaming. This was followed by gunshots.

"What the—" Trent said as a bullet punched in and out of the tent, buzzing between them as it went.

"Jesus," Brandy said, as they scrambled out of the tent, keeping low to the ground.

Chapter 5

The roaring stopped, but the screaming contin-ued, as well as the gunshots. Trent and Brandy crouched low outside of their tent. Trent pointed past the fire toward the tree line. "Something just ran into the trees over there."

"Over there too," Brandy said, pointing in the oppo-site direction. "Looks like *two* somethings."

A bullet buzzed past them, nicking the fire and sending up a spray of sparks.

"What is he even shooting at?" Brandy said.

Trent shouted, "Dibble. Hey, Dibble. Cool it."

Another gunshot kicked up dirt a yard from Trent and Brandy.

"Christ. Please stop," Trent shouted.

"Who goes there?" Dibble shouted back.

"It's Trent and Dr. Phillips. Please stop shooting at us."

"Please stop shooting in general," Norm shouted from his tent.

The girls' screaming had turned to sobbing.

"We're coming to the campfire," Trent called. "Don't shoot at us."

"Don't shoot in general," Norm added.

"Okay, we rally at the Alpha Point," Deputy Dibble called.

"What the fuck's the Alpha Point?" Trent asked Brandy.

"The fire, I guess?" Brandy said.

"What the fuck is the Alpha Point?" Norm called.

"The fire," Brandy called. "Rally at the fire."

Trent, Brandy, and Norm gathered around the fire. The dude ducked his head out of his tent and joined them. Deputy Dibble danced his way toward them, weaving to the fire, pointing his firearm in every direction like a bird's head darting for signs of danger.

"Will you stop pointing that thing at us?" Trent said.

"Maybe stop pointing it in general?" Norm said.

"Where's Quint?" Brandy said.

"Don't know," Deputy Dibble said.

"Where are the girls?" Brandy said.

"In the tent crying," the dude said, rubbing his shoulders to ward off the cold.

"Where's Burke?" Trent said.

"In the tent crying," Norm said.

"It's fucking freezing," the dude said, intensifying his rubbing and jumping up and down.

"You're not wearing any clothes," Trent said.

"Ew," Brandy said.

"Please stop jumping," Norm said.

"Shit," the dude said.

There was a snap of a twig and Deputy Dibble raised his gun again.

"Will you stop pointing that thing at us?" Trent said.

"Tell him that too," Norm said, pointing at the dude.

"Can you please put some clothes on?" Brandy said.

"Oh yeah," the dude said and darted for his tent.

Deputy Dibble pointed his weapon toward another snapping twig, and when something burst through the underbrush, Trent had to knock Dibble's arms down. Dibble fired into the ground, inches from Trent's feet.

"Jesus, will you cool it?" Trent shouted, and then pointed at two figures emerging from the woods. "It's Quint."

"Who's that with him?" Brandy said.

"Is that the Bigfoot?" Dibble said.

"Does that look like a Bigfoot?" Trent said.

A young, wiry man walked in front of Quint. Quint had the barrel of his shotgun jammed into the young man's back.

"No," Dibble said. "It looks like…"

The dude came out of the tent and said, "Daryl."

Dibble said, "Daryl Jackson, quarterback of the local college."

"What college is that?" Brandy said.

"The one right close by," Dibble said.

"You know him?" Trent said to the dude.

"Shit," the dude said.

"So let me get this straight," Trent said to the dude, "You convinced this knucklehead," he gestured toward

Daryl, who was still being held at shotgun point, "to come out here and pretend to be a Bigfoot to scare the girls into a threesome with you?"

The girls suddenly appeared from their tents.

"What?" the brunette said.

"You asshole," the blonde said.

"It's really cold," the brunette said, rubbing her shoulders and jumping up and down.

"You're not wearing any clothes," Brandy said.

"Whoops," the brunette said.

"Hey, I'm not either," the blonde said.

"It's actually not that cold," Norm said.

"Yeah, it's balmy even," Trent said.

"Why don't you go get some clothes on, girls," Brandy said.

"I think they'll be fine," Norm said.

"Girls," Brandy said. "Clothes."

"Oh, yeah," the brunette said, and the girls ducked back into the tent.

"Damn," Norm said.

"Back to the threesome," Brandy said.

"Yeah, so about the threesome," Trent said. "You really thought you could scare the girls into…?"

"No," Brandy said, "the threesome of knuckleheads. Daryl said there were three of them."

"Where are the other two?" Trent said.

"Little minnows swam off that'a way," Quint said, pointing into the woods.

"Did you just say little minnows?" Norm said.

The dude said, "I thought it would be funny. You know, having them pretend to be a Bigfoot and all? I tried to send a text message to stop them, but there's no service out here."

"Quint, what's the chances of those other knuckleheads finding their way out of this forest at night, running away from the trail?" Brandy said.

"They got a better chance of a shark attack out here," Quint said.

Norm rolled his eyes.

"How big is this forest if they get lost?" Brandy said.

"700 square miles," Quint said.

"So if they run in a straight line, they'll just come out eventually, right?" Deputy Dibble said. "Isn't that, like, physics?"

Quint began singing, "*Farewell and adieu, you….*" He stopped and looked at Norm, who was staring and smiling at Daryl. Everyone turned to look at Norm.

Norm seemed to break from his thoughts. "Huh?" he said. "Oh, sorry, I was distracted."

Trent nodded toward Daryl and said to Norm, "You know him or something?"

"No," Norm said. "But he's Black."

"So?" Daryl said.

"Look, sorry," Norm said. "It's just that now I'm not the only minority, and everyone knows the Black guy goes first. I got, like, a reprieve."

Brandy said, "I don't think race is a mitigating factor for animal attacks."

"Mitigating factors don't matter," Norm said. "Haven't you ever seen a horror movie? Minorities always go first. But Black guys supersede Asians in order of death."

"That's true," Daryl said. "Damn it."

"This isn't a movie," Trent said.

"I think the rules still apply," Daryl said. "Shit, what do I do?"

Brandy said, "But everyone who has died so far has been white."

"It's about odds," Norm said. "As a minority, my odds of biting it were the highest."

Daryl said, "And now my odds of biting it are the highest."

Burke rolled up to the fire. "Norm," he said. "You need to run out there and get the camera traps."

"Fuck," Norm said.

"Hey," Daryl said, "In horror movie rules, doesn't leaving the group, like, trump being Black? This increases *his* odds of biting it, right? Reprieve is mine now."

Quint began singing, "*Farewell and adieu…*"

Norm and Quint walked through the inky darkness of the forest. Norm sliced through the night's membrane with a flashlight. Quint had a light strapped to the barrel of his shotgun.

"Thanks for coming out here with me," Norm said.

"Couldn't let catnip like you out here for the bears to eat," Quint said.

"So you do think it was a bear that attacked those students?"

"Who knows?" Quint said.

"But obviously it isn't a Bigfoot," Norm said.

"Son, there be a lot of strange stuff out here in these woods. I seen strange lights in the sky, apparitions of First Nation Indians, giant winged creatures flying through the trees, even once seen what looked and sounded like a tiger roaring. And, yes, I seen huge, humanoid figures stalking through the trees."

"But you're also a drunk."

"This is true."

"So it was most likely a bear that attacked those campers."

"Yep."

They walked a little ways, fighting the dark.

After the silence was thicker than the darkness, Norm said, "I can't believe I got conned into all this."

"People don't get conned into things. It be blinders of desire that get them to do what they do."

"Sorry, I don't have my Quint to English dictionary right now. Care to elaborate?"

"You wanted something, Burke offered something. It's the end result that determines if it be worth it or not. If the end result isn't what you expected, it be a con in your mind."

"This from the hunter who got conned out here to shoot a Bigfoot."

"I be getting paid to hunt this here Bigfoot."

"A Bigfoot that doesn't exist."

Quint shrugged. "End result is the money. What do I care if it be a Bigfoot or not? If I get paid, then who got conned? You be getting paid for pushing that twerp through these here woods?"

"No."

"Then you weren't conned, son; you're just stupid."

"I don't *technically* get paid. I get credit for the internship."

"Will you still get that credit?"

"Yes."

"Then you got paid."

"But I didn't actually *learn* anything."

"Seems you be learning plenty."

They walked in silence for a few minutes.

"Why do they call you Quint?" Norm said.

"Because when I was young, I had the best Quint-sanera for miles."

"But you're not Mexican."

"How do you know?"

"Because if you were, you'd know it's *Quinceanera*. And they're for girls."

Quint turned the barrel of his shotgun to a nook in a tree. A box was illuminated in the light. "That your camera trap?"

"Yep."

"Let's grab it and get back to camp. We be chum out here."

"I'm really starting to hate you."

———————————

The group, now gathered like a football huddle, peeked over Burke's shoulder at the monitor in his lap.

"What exactly are we watching for here?" Trent said.

"Does it matter?" Norm said. "I risked my life to get this thing, even if it's *The Real Housewives*, we're watching it."

Deputy Dibble said, "Aw, man, is that on tonight?"

"I'm just trying to understand what exactly we're looking for," Trent said.

"Aren't we looking for the Bigfoot?" Deputy Dibble said.

"But we know the Bigfoot was just the dude's friends," Trent said.

"Maybe we can get some indication of where the dude's friends are going," Brandy said.

"They're long gone by now," Trent said.

"They're long lost by now," Norm said.

"They could be going in circles out there," Brandy said. "Maybe this can tell us."

"I still don't see the point of this scene," Trent said.

"Did you just say scene?" Norm asked.

"Maybe there'll be, like, a big reveal of a sas-squash," Deputy Dibble said.

"Squatch," Brandy said.

Deputy Dibble squatted, saying, "Sorry, can you not see or something?"

"No, it's—" Brandy began, but Burke interrupted her.

"Look, there." Burke pointed at the screen.

On the screen, three young men, tinted green by the camera's night vision, wandered past the camera. Daryl was in the lead.

"Hey, that's you," Deputy Dibble said to Daryl.

One of the men behind Daryl was sleek and agile looking, the other large and lumbering.

"That's Flash and Lug," the blonde girl said.

"Why did you bring Lug?" the dude asked Daryl.

Daryl shrugged. "Said he wanted to come."

"Why? What's wrong with Lug?" Norm said.

"He's so dumb," the blonde girl said, rolling her eyes.

On the screen, the three men had gone past the camera, and now there was just forest.

"I guess we should fast forward and see if we see them come back around?" Brandy said.

"No Bigfoot?" Deputy Dibble said.

"Burke, fast forward this thing," Trent said.

Brandy said, "Sorry, Deputy Dibble, but there is no Bigf—"

"Whoa, wait, what is that?" Norm said, pointing at the screen.

A wall of hair passed the camera.

"What the hell…?" Daryl said.

"Rewind that," Brandy said.

Burke rewound the video. The hairy figure passed in front of the camera again.

"Can anyone make out any discernible features?" Brandy said.

"Is hair a discernible feature?" Deputy Dibble said.

"It looked like it was walking upright," Brandy said. "But it was far too tall for any primate I know of."

"Including human," Trent said quietly.

"Quint," Brandy said, "That look like a bear to you?"

"Hair look like a bear," Quint said. "And size too. But don't know many bears walking upright like that."

"Its shoulders were back," Trent said.

Brandy turned to the dude and Daryl and said, "Did anyone else come out here with you? Maybe in a costume or something?"

"No," Daryl said. "Just me, Flash, and Lug."

"Maybe it was Lug with his shirt off," the blonde said. "He's real hairy."

"Isn't he bald?" Norm said.

"No. He shaves his head," the blonde said. "The rest of him is real hairy."

"How do you know?" the brunette asked her.

"Because he asked me to shave his back for him. It took a really long time."

Norm said, "But if you shaved it, then how could he still be hairy…? You know what, never mind."

"Maybe now you'll all believe me about the Squatch Wars," Burke said.

"Squatch Wars," Deputy Dibble said in his monster truck voice.

"It has to be an illusion," Trent said. "Some kind of forced perspective on the camera. For all we know, a squirrel darted in front of the lens."

"Or there's something very large following those kids," Brandy said.

"But then they came here, and they were fine," Trent said.

"Did they know something was following them?" Brandy said.

"What if they were making all that noise because they knew they were in danger and were trying to get into the tent for safety?" Norm said.

"You know, I'm right here," Daryl said. "You can just ask me what happened."

"Oh yeah," Brandy said.

"So what happened?" Trent said.

"We hiked out here. Drank a shitload of beers. And then came to scare y'all," Daryl said.

"That was very succinct," Trent said.

 Brandy said, "You didn't hear anything behind you?"

"I heard something crashing behind me and then Lug goes running ahead of us screaming toward the tents, so I figured it was him that did the crashing. Then y'all started shooting at us and we ran back into the woods."

"And your friends are now most likely lost and wandering hundreds of square miles," Brandy said.

Norm looked at Quint. "No farewell and adieu?"

"I thought that be obvious," Quint said.

"How obvious?" Norm said.

"Those boys be fucked," Quint said.

"And there's another issue," Trent said. "There is a very large animal out there."

"A squatch," Burke said.

"And they led it right here," Brandy said. "Which means…."

Norm and Quint both said, "We're gonna need a bigger boat."

Two flashlight beams cut through the blackness of the deep forest, the lights dancing and bouncing off tree trunks. One light stopped on a ribbon tied to a tree branch.

"Look here, son, I told you I'd find the trail," Flash said.

"Why you keep calling me son?" Lug said. "I never get why you do that."

"It's a term of dis-endearment, used when dumb motherfuckers like you doubt smart motherfuckers like me. Of course, me being a receiver and you a lineman, it's no wonder I understand routes and directions far better than your dumb ass. Now let's go. Start looking for more ribbons. A trail's got to be leading somewhere."

"Yeah, back to the camp where people were shooting at us."

"That was obviously a misunderstanding we will clear up. I don't know who those people were with

Dude, but I bet they know the way out of here. Either that, or we find our way out on our own."

"How do you even know this is the trail?"

"Because of this ribbon here," Flash said, caressing the cloth. "I saw ribbons tied to trees on the way in here earlier. So come on."

They began walking.

"How do you know they mark a trail?" Lug said. "There might just be random ribbons tied to trees all over the forest."

"What? You think bears are out here sprucing up the place? Son, please."

"Could be from an inbred family of psychopaths with hooks and chainsaws, looking to make masks out of our faces," Lug said.

"Number one, no one is going to want your face for a mask, and number two, no white motherfucker is going to catch me," Flash said.

"How you know they're white?"

"Because inbred psychopaths with chainsaws are always white. And they're always slow, so they ain't going to catch me."

"Or even find you in this dark."

"See? Why do you have to go all racist on me like that?"

"I wasn't. Your skin is dark. And it's dark out. How is that racist? It's like an asset in this situation. I was paying you a compliment. Why do you think everything I say is racist?"

"Because most of the shit you say is racist."

"Like what?"

"I don't know. Like everything." Flash said. "Basically, you open your mouth, you can bet something racist is coming out."

"*Everything* I say is racist?"

"Well…like dick size, for example. You're always bringing up dick size with me and Daryl, like Black people are the authority on dick sizes or something."

"Well, it's another good asset you got. How is it insulting to say you have a big dick?"

"I don't know. Maybe it's just a tic or something, because every white boy does it. It comes off as racist."

"Not because I mean it to be."

"It's just dumb, is all."

"Don't call me dumb."

"Then don't be dumb."

"You're dumb."

"No, you're dumb."

"You're dumb."

"No, you're—we aren't getting anywhere with this. Let's hug it out."

"Hug it out, bitch."

Flash and Lug embraced.

"All right," Flash said after their hug ended, "let's see if I can get your dumb ass out of here."

"See, you're calling me dumb, and—"

"We hugged it out, stop bitching—hold on, look. There's another ribbon. And see, this one is pink. You think some inbred, chainsaw wielding psychopath is gonna use a pink ribbon?"

"Could be a faded piece of their confederate flag."

"Some racist not gonna cut up their confederate flag. That's like using a page of a bible to roll a spliff."

"Could be the shirt of some girl they killed. Or some homo like you. I seen you wearing pink."

"I wear pink because I make pink look good. But be smart; you think they dumb enough to hang the clothes of a murder victim out here for the police to find? Even mindless murderers aren't that dumb."

"Maybe they're doing it to taunt the police."

"Man, I knew you dumb, but I didn't think you were dumber than any inbred motherfu—" Flash stopped and cocked his head. "You hear that?"

"All I hear is you saying stupid shit. Because you're dumb."

"No, you're dumb."

"Better than stupid."

"I'd rather be stupid than—"

"Hug it out?"

"Hug it out, bitch."

The two embraced. Then Flash swept the night with his flashlight beam. "Hey, yo, another ribbon."

Their pace quickened.

"I can't believe Dude conned us into coming out here," Lug said. "I'm gonna wreck that fucker."

"He didn't con you, fool; *you* volunteered. In fact, you were pissed he didn't ask you and then you demanded for us to take you."

"It was like some Jedi mind trick or something, telling me not to come. It conned me into coming."

"Son, you really are dumber than some Leatherface inbred."

"Stop calling me *son*."

"Then stop acting like a child."

"*You're* a child," Lug said.

"Man, I hate to see what all them concussions are doing to your brain," Flash said.

"I don't get concussions, man. I can take a hit from a wrecking ball and not go down."

"Just because you don't go down doesn't mean it ain't scrambling your brain."

"Don't talk to me about scrambled brains with all that shit you smoke," Lug said. "Only reason you're out here is because Dude gets you your gange, mon."

"And you your roids," Flash said.

"I'm not on roids."

"If you say so. And, see? Saying, *gange, mon*, is racist."

"I'm just stating a fact. He gets you your shit."

"At least taking care of my dealer is a better reason than coming out here trying to catch a glimpse of some naked-ass blonde girl. Like you'd ever have a shot with her."

"I think I caught a glimpse of her tit when I tried getting in the tent."

"And that's another thing," Flash said. "What you doing trying to get into the tent? We supposed to be just hitting on the sides. And you were, like, screaming for them to let you in."

"I heard something behind us. I think it was a bear or something."

"Wasn't no bear. Bears don't hunt at night. It was probably like a fox or a chipmunk or something, and you run off screaming."

"How you know bears don't hunt at night?"

"I learned it in my ecology class."

"That class is bullshit. And I didn't run off screaming," Lug said. "I ran to warn Dude and the chicks that there was a bear out there. I was being a hero."

"Son, I heard you cry—wait, you hear that?"

"You fucking with me now? Keep saying you hearing things so I get scared?" Lug said.

"Nah, man, I hear snapping twigs. Might be your hook and chainsaw men. Or the nocturnal bears you scared of. Whatever it is, I notice you been walking in the back all night."

"I'm walking in the back because you claim you know where you're going. But I ain't scared of no inbreds or bears or nothing, because unlike your skinny bitch arms, I can actually kick some ass. So look out." Lug nudged Flash aside and strode in the lead, shouting, "C'mon you motherfucking bears, you want a piece of me?"

"Stop being dumb," Flash said.

"You're being dumb."

"No you're—hug it out?"

"Hug it out, bit—"

Before he could finish, something large and hairy dropped from the trees in front of Lug. The thing—which looked like a giant ape or bear or even man—grabbed Lug's arm and ran toward a tree. It smacked Lug against the bark with a sickening thud. Lug's arm dislodged from his body at the shoulder, but he didn't fall. He stood, half of his facial bones recessed, one eye now uselessly gazing in the wrong direction, blood spurting from the severed brachial artery in his shoulder.

The giant animal regarded the still upright Lug with curiosity before grabbing Lug's head and pounding his face against the tree three times. The animal slammed its foot on the ground with each hit as if to intensify the thudding, then it looked on curiously as Lug still stood upright—now, both the lineman's eyes stared uselessly in opposite directions.

A small squeak rose in the silence of the woods, and the giant animal turned toward Flash. Flash stood frozen, and as his eyes met the animal's, he let out another squeak. The giant animal, still holding Lug's disembodied arm, strode toward Flash. Flash could only regard the thing awash in his flashlight's beam; his body would not follow his brain's commands to run.

The giant regarded Flash in much the same manner it had regarded Lug, with a mix of curiosity and examination. It then swung Lug's arm like a club. The end of the arm smacked Flash on top of his head and made a hollow squishing sound like someone dropping meat onto a counter. Blood smeared Flash's forehead. "Ouch," Flash said, rubbing the top of his head.

The thing inspected the arm, as if for a defect, and tossed it aside. It then raised its hands to its ears and thumped its chest.

A rivulet of Lug's blood dripped over the edge of Flash's brow and then between his eye and nose like a tear. Flash rubbed the bloody tear away, and this action broke him from his paralysis; his brain finally registered what was happening. He needed to run, and when Flash ran, no one and no thing could catch him.

He said, "Just try and catch me, motherfucker," as he turned and took off with the speed which had bestowed him with his nickname. He felt the rising freedom of a stallion on an open plain as trees darted by him, but then he tripped on a root and tumbled to the ground. His flashlight's beam skittered off ahead of him. He scrambled to get to his feet, feeling the darkness materialize with tangible weight above him. Looking up, the last thing to go through his mind was a giant elbow.

Chapter 6

The campsite's fire was now smoldering embers. The sun blotched the ground in kaleidoscopic arrays. Deputy Dibble sat, snoring, beside the fire.

"There's our last line of defense," Brandy said, nodding toward the sleeping lawman.

"Glad nothing else came by," Trent said. "I'm guessing that's how Daryl and his friends slipped into camp in the first place."

"There was never any danger," Quint said. Brandy and Trent turned to find the hunter with his shotgun held in the crook of his arm. "I made sure nothing be close."

"You were awake when I had watch," Trent said.

"He was awake during my watch too," Norm said, arriving beside the fire, rubbing his eyes.

"Mine too," Brandy said. "Did you sleep at all last night, Quint?"

"I was able to get my fifty winks," Quint said.

"Isn't it forty winks?" Brandy said.

"It's fifty for him," Norm said. "That's why they call him Quint."

"Now you're getting it, laddie," Quint said.

"Hey, Deputy Dibble," Trent said, nudging the deputy with his foot. "Time to—"

Deputy Dibble leapt up with his sidearm drawn. Trent had just enough time to knock the weapon up so it fired into the air.

"Jesus Christ," Trent shouted. "You point that thing at one more person and I'm taking it away."

"Geez, sorry," Dibble said. "Why'd you sneak up on me like that?"

"Sneak? We've all been standing here having a conversation for like ten minutes," Norm said.

Daryl, Dude, and the girls came running to the fire.

"We heard a gunshot," Dude said. "Are Flash and Lug back?"

"No. It was a misfire," Brandy said.

"Deputy Dawg can't keep it in his pants," Trent said.

Norm regarded the college students. "You're wearing clothes."

"Yeah, well, we assume we're heading back?" Dude said.

"And we have to take our pictures for the shrine," the blonde said.

"Is there a way you all could, like, move to one side, so you don't ruin the pictures?" the brunette said.

"We should discuss what to do next. The logical thing is to return to the sheriff's station," Trent said.

"We stay," Burke said, wheeling up to the group. "We came out here to find the squatch. And we have. Now we stay and study it."

"We can't keep them out here," Brandy said, motioning to the college students.

"They don't have to stay," Burke said. "They found their way out here; they can find their way back."

"And we have to take our pictures," the blonde said.

"We have to report the two who are missing," Brandy said.

"They can do that too," Burke said, motioning at the students around the fire.

"What we saw on that camera was most likely a bear," Brandy said. "Why would we stay out here with a bear nearby?"

"It was a sasquatch," Burke said.

"Why would we stay here with a sasquatch nearby?" Norm said.

"Why would we stay here with no other Black people nearby?" Daryl said.

"That was no bear," Burke said. "That was the distinct nocturnal hunting of a sasquatch."

Brandy said, "Quint, do bears hunt at night?"

"If they be hungry enough."

"See?" Brandy said. "Why would we stay out here with a *hungry* bear?"

"If the bear was hungry," Trent said, "then why didn't it eat any of the victims the other night?"

"Jesus, whose side are you on?" Brandy said.

"The truth's," Trent said.

"You think it's a Bigfoot?"

"I think…you know what I think."

"A human?" Brandy said. "Then you want to stay out here with a psychopathic human?"

"Human?" Norm said. "What's this about a human?"

"He thinks it's Rad Rocky Hollywood," Brandy said.

"The wrestler?" Norm said.

"How do you know Rad Rocky?" Brandy said. "You're way too young for that."

"I'm a know-it-all nerd," Norm said. "I know everything."

"Don't need to be no nerd to know Rad Rocky," Dude said.

"Yeah, he was pretty badass," Daryl said.

Dude put his hands to his ears and then thumped his chest before pretending to pile drive an elbow into Daryl's shoulder.

Trent motioned toward them, saying to Brandy, "See? The move?"

Brandy rolled her eyes. "We need to go back and report to the sheriff. Find out what he wants to do."

Norm said to Deputy Dibble, "Don't you have, like, a radio or something? Couldn't we just call and ask him?"

"My radio," Dibble said, smacking his head. "I forgot my damn radio at the station. I should go back to get that thing."

"Would've been safer if he'd forgotten his gun," Norm said.

"Looks like it's settled. We're heading back to the sheriff's station," Trent said.

———————————

The group broke camp and made their way through the woods and toward the main trail. Norm fought Burke's wheelchair over a large root. Burke sat still in his chair, pouting.

"I don't know why you're the one sulking," Norm said. "Can you maybe make your weight just a little less dead?"

"But I *am* dead," Burke said. "Dead inside. We're this close to a squatch, and we leave."

"If it makes you feel any better," Norm said, "there's no such thing as a sasquatch."

Burke sank deeper in his chair, his weight becoming deader.

"Probably shoulda told him that after you got him over that root," Quint said.

"You could help, you know."

"Hands are full," the hunter said, holding up his shotgun and flask.

Norm muscled the chair over the obstacle. Quint held the flask toward him, offering him a drink.

"What is that stuff?" Norm said.

"Perfect Pitch," Quint said.

"Is that, like, some metaphorical statement that is supposed to mean something to me?" Norm said.

From ahead of them, Trent called over his shoulder, "It's a type of moonshine. Made from pine trees. Shit will make you go blind."

"I'm all set, thanks," Norm said, holding up his hand to decline the offer.

"Suit yourself," Quint said as he took a swig from the flask.

"How is that thing not empty by now?" Norm said, nodding toward the flask.

Quint held open his jacket. Several pockets had been added to the inside lining, each of them holding a flask.

Norm stared in disbelief. "Holy shit."

Trent said, "You know, authorities have been trying to find the Perfect Pitch distributor for years. A few months back the stuff just disappeared off the market, and yet here you are with all these flasks full of it. You don't strike me as the saving-for-a-rainy-day kind of guy, Quint. Where did you get all of those?"

"Found em," Quint said.

"Uh-huh," Trent said, his voice thick with skepticism.

Brandy said, in a low voice out of the corner of her mouth, "Is it smart to accuse a possible moonshiner holding a shotgun in the middle of deep woods?"

"I wasn't accusing, just pointing out the facts," Trent said. "That's my job."

"Why do you drink that shit?" Norm asked Quint.

Quint looked off at distant trees, his eyes focusing on a time long ago. He said, "Flashback to Laos, 1971, and a little thing called Lam Son 719."

"You were a part of Lam Son?" Trent said.

"Flashback?" Norm said.

"Yup, I was a part of it." Quint said.

"Who is Lam Son?" Brandy said.

"Isn't that the name of that Asian guy in our biology class?" Dude asked Daryl.

"That guy's name is Harold," Daryl said.

"Lam Son isn't a who; it's a what," Trent said.

"Okay, then what is Lam Son?" Brandy said.

"It was an operation by the South Vietnamese during the war," Trent said. "They were on the Laos border trying to stop the flow of supplies along the Ho Chi Minh Trail. It was one of the bloodiest operations of the war. Technically the U.S. was only there for air support."

"I was part of a four-man Huey crew," Quint said. "Gunner I was. We was providing air support, but our objective was limited at the time because we had some know-it-all reporter embedded with us."

Everyone turned and looked at Trent.

"What?" Trent said. "I wasn't there."

Quint continued. "We was supposed to stay along the perimeter of a deep jungle forest. Watch for any Charl—" He glanced at Norm. "Any enemy activity coming out of that tree-line. I'd fire off rounds of the M-60, basically firing at nothing. Just to give the reporter something to see and write about. Let him feel the percussive waves of that big gun going off, combined with the thudding of the rotors…it be like a symphony. But that reporter thought he know it all. Was the type that had an explanation for everything. Thought he be smarter than us crew and telling the pilot what to do. You know the type."

They all looked at Trent again.

"He's not talking about me," Trent said. "I wasn't even born yet in 1971."

Quint continued. "Reporter keep goading the pilot to fly over the jungle. Says he wants a sense of what it be like to look down upon an impenetrable surface, like looking upon the green of a deep sea, not privy to the life and dangers below."

"Oh, that's pretty good," Trent said, taking his notebook from his pocket.

"But there be dangers below us. Out there, under that sea of green, there be monsters a plenty."

Trent nodded and smiled, and continued writing.

"Sun was low in the sky, due to the coming night," Quint said, "so we didn't see the first tracers streak past the chopper. It was when the reporter's foot exploded in a burst of blood that we realized the fuselage had been hit. Reporter didn't scream at first. He just looked at me with his face freckled red, looking like some confused kid questioning the facts of life. Only answer I had for him was one word: *Incoming.*"

Those gathered around Quint jumped as he shouted the word.

"The chopper was suddenly belching streams of white smoke and spewing an acrid smell, which be a bad sign, but then that smoke roiled to black, and that be death. Meant the engine was about to quit and we'd be dropping out of the sky like a present down the chimney, either being killed by the impact, or wrapped up with a bow for them goo—" He glanced at Norm again. "Vietcong," Quint said. "Amazingly, we lost our tail rotor then, which is usually a death sentence in itself, but the sudden spinning of the fuselage created an energy feedback for the rotor and gave us enough momentum to skitter along the treetops and out of the immediate reach of those Cong that brought us down. The spinning was dizzying, the setting sun bursting in and out of the open bay doors like a strobe light, and I remember that reporter started screaming then and only stopped when he puked right onto his bloody, mangled foot. Even in that death spin, all I could think about was the rot that would be growing on that reporter's foot within a day, and how that foot was as good as gone that instant."

"Gnarly," Dude whispered.

"Our relief was short-lived," Quint continued. "Though we'd bought some time spinning away from the Cong, we still had to contend with the landing, and," here Quint took a second before continuing, "not all of us be that fortunate." He took a swig from his flask. "The chopper spun into the trees. The rotor was still turning, cleaving the foliage like a lawn mower, and branches poked through the doors, just missing us like we be the girl in a magician's sword box trick. We all dropped to the chopper's floor to avoid being impaled, but with the pitch of the aircraft, the other gunner, Larry O'Shea—we called him Lucky—slid out one of the doors, and I swear, as if in slow motion, I see him cut in half by the rotor and disappear below us."

Brandy gasped and covered her mouth. Dude and Daryl looked at each other wide-eyed. Trent continued writing.

"The rest of us were lucky for those branches, though, for in another few seconds, they stopped the rotor and they stopped the spinning, and then like loving hands those branches passed us from one tree to the next, gently laying us down on the jungle floor like a momma laying her baby on a blanket."

Trent's head was nodding like he was listening to jazz, and a wry smile slipped across his face as he wrote.

"We sat stunned for a moment, the engine coughing out its final acrid puffs," Quint said. "And the silence was complete. That's the thing, be it forest or jungle, the silence is a complete silence, them trees gather up noises like a child gathering up jacks. But that silence didn't last long as the reporter began wailing, a low guttural sound. The sound of a child who didn't believe in monsters, but now discovered that they be real. This sound seemed to dispel the shock, made it real for us crew, so we sprang to action. We needed to get as far away from this wreck as possible, because Ch—the enemy was on the way. We gathered our gear and the reporter and climbed from the chopper. With the sun setting, the jungle was rapidly darkening. And it was there the silence gave up another sound. A gasping groan. We turned to find Lucky, his entrails dragging from his stomach as he clawed the top half of his body toward the bottom half several feet away from him, trying to gather himself back whole."

Dude and Daryl looked at each other and both said, "Whoa."

Trent whistled and continued writing.

Burke threw up a little and swallowed it, burning on its way back down.

Quint said, "The pilot, who we called Providence cause of where he from, knelt over Lucky, turning him over. While Prov told Lucky he was gonna be okay, I slipped my sidearm from its holster. Lucky wasn't gonna be okay, and I knew I'd probably be court martialed for it, but I wasn't letting Lucky go out like he was going out. I pointed that .45 right between Lucky's eyes, and those eyes fell on me, and a smile crept across his mouth, and I swear that smile even crept into his eyes until all light faded from them and I know he be gone. And even though I ended up not needing to pull that trigger, at least he went knowing his friend was going to do what it take for him."

Brandy wiped a tear from her eye. Burke did too.

Quint continued, "We know we need to get to the tree line. Prov had issued a mayday, and there weren't no way another chopper would risk flying over that jungle canopy. We also know we have only so much time before the napalm be dropping to eliminate those hidden anti-aircraft guns. Thing is, finding one's way in a jungle at night can be difficult.

Not like ya have any celestial guidance, and turning on the flashlight to check the compass only gives your position to th—those seeking to destroy you. Usually, you stay where you are and wait for morning before you travel, but we couldn't do that. We needed to move south, but not directly south, or we'd just meet our pursuers half way. We came up with a plan, and stayed disciplined. We used the flashlight for five-second increments, long enough to check the compass and the landscape ahead of us. Prov stayed on the left, memorizing what he see on his side. The copilot, Willy Miller, who we called Milky Way, watched the right. I had the reporter, helping him walk on his mangled foot while the pilot and copilot led us through the blackness for one hundred pace intervals. Then we turn on that light for five more seconds and move along again. We were making it along pretty good, hopefully keeping the light from giving us away. But, of course, there be other hunters in that jungle, and ones that don't need light to find us. The first tiger came around midnight."

Trent finally looked up from his pad. "I'm sorry, tiger? Like tiger-tiger?"

"A-yep," Quint said. "Tiger-tiger. Like the big pussy cat."

"Whoa," Dude and Daryl said again.

"We stopped for one of our compass checks," Quint said, "and suddenly Prov was just gone. Like some kind of *Beam me up, Spocky* situation."

"Scotty," Norm said. "It's beam me up—" When every-one turned toward him, he said, "Not the right time."

"That's the thing about ambush predators," Quint said. "People think there's some kind of warning—a growl, or spotting an animal crouched waiting in front of you along the path. There's none of that. You have no idea that a tiger is anywhere nearby. It is so still it literally be just part of the forest until it don't want to be no more, and then it silently takes you. Not even a scream from Providence, because that cat already have him by the jugular."

Quint took a swig from his flask and regarded the woods around him for a moment.

"The smart thing," he said, "would have been to stop and build a fire. Wait until that cat—or those cats; we have no idea how many there be—moved on, but we couldn't risk stopping and being POWed, so we's kept moving, but we did risk keeping the flashlights on, because now we fought the night, and the night had teeth."

Trent scribbled frantically in his notebook again.

"We continue on for about an hour. Lights on, sidearms drawn. I gave my flashlight to the reporter, given my free hand was propping him up. This bc disorienting, trying to watch for something and the light not adhering to your sightline. So the light was facing the opposite way when Milky Way was taken. He was just gone in the darkness, but I had enough time to spot his flashlight disappear into the branches, flashing like a signal lamp calling a final SOS before being gone completely. And then it was the two of us, me and that reporter. I gave him my sidearm and threw that lad over my shoulder in a fireman's carry, telling him to shoot at anything he thought be coming out of those woods, and me, holding the flashlight, just ran like I was Forest-fucking-Gump."

The group had gravitated closer to Quint, all their shoulders touching now. All, that is, except for Trent, who continued scribbling in his notebook, and Burke, who was left outside the huddle in his wheelchair.

"My hope was that the tiger now had his fill. Tigers don't generally hunt in packs, and to this day, I still don't know if it be one, or if those woods just be so full of cats that night that we be like a Golden Corral for the beasts. Maybe our chopper crashing be a dinner bell for every tiger in the area. But, alas, whether one cat or one hundred, I ran, even with that heavy sack of shit slung over my shoulder, until suddenly that weight be gone. Gone without even a single gunshot. With that weight gone, I tumbled to the ground, and when I scrambled to get up, I spotted the beast crouched over its newly obtained prize, its teeth sunk into the reporter's throat. Both the cat and the reporter staring up at me. The reporter's eyes dilated so wide their black almost took over the whites. The tiger's eyes glowed green in the flashlight's beam. That's the thing about the eye of the tiger, it's the look of one who knows all, as if understanding every mistake you ever made in life, and every mistake you're going to make."

Trent paused only to flip the page over in his notebook and then continued scribbling as fast as he could.

"I began edging backward, keeping eye contact with that beast, knowing the second I broke my gaze from its, it would be upon me. When the reporter stopped twitching and those eyes of his went slack, the beast raised its head and let out a roar. It be a sound felt rather than heard. Like the rotors of the chopper or the M60 ringing out, it was a vibration of unspeakable power, a harbinger of annihilation."

"Hold on," Trent said, holding up a finger, trying to scribble the last words spoken.

"No hold on," Brandy said. "Speak, damn it."

Quint took a swig from his flask. "I backed up slowly, keeping that eye contact, and the tiger lowered and tensed, its tail twitching. I knew it be about to pounce. I figured maybe I could shine the light directly into its eyes, or even throw the whole flashlight at it to distract it enough to make a break for it, but I knew making a break for it was the last thing I should do, so I just kept edging away. I took step after step into the dark, until one step opened into an abyss, and with a rollercoaster heart-drop of surprise, I was tumbling down a steep embankment. Felt like I be tumbling for miles, but was really about 100 yards. And at the end of those hundred yards, I tumbled into a river and was rushed away on the current. Before I lost my flashlight, I swore I could see those glowing eyes at the top of the embankment, staring down with that eerie intelligence. I know tigers be great swimmers, but I couldn't imagine that cat would leave its other three kills to brave those waters. So I lay back, looking up at a lightening sky, allowing those waters to baptize me to safety, which they did. They rushed me out of the hot zone. And when I saw the choppers circling above me like vultures, I gave into my fate, and allowed them to take me home. There I took a drink, and I haven't stopped since. That was March 23, 1971, when four men be taken by the jungle, and the fifth be left to walk his waking death."

There was silence. Then Norm swallowed and said in a croaking voice, "Is that why they call you Quint?"

Quint shook his head slowly. "No."

"That was quite a story," Trent said.

"Long," Dude said.

"And boring," the brunette said.

"And uncharacteristically eloquent," Brandy said.

"Were there even many '*be*'s in that story?" Norm said.

"I thought they were tigers," the blonde said.

"Hey, wait a minute," Deputy Dibble said, "You know, the sheriff's been looking for the distributor of Perfect Pitch, and Quint has so much of it."

Everyone turned to look at Deputy Dibble.

Trent said, "Yeah, we talked about that, like—"

Something large and moaning broke from the trees.

Deputy Dibble's gun was up in a flash and he fired two shots.

"Whoa," Dude said. "You just shot Lug."

"You bastard," the blonde screamed.

Chapter 7

"Give me the gun," Trent said to Dibble.

Deputy Dibble handed over the gun to Trent. "Gee, sorry," he said.

"Whoa," Dude said. "You blew his arm off."

Brandy bent over Lug. "There's no way these injuries were made by that gun. His arm has been torn off and his face bashed in."

"You gone do that boy a favor, lad," Quint said to Dibble. "Putting him out of his misery you did."

"He's not dead," Brandy said, checking his pulse.

"Yay," the blonde said.

"Is it even possible to survive all of these injuries?" Trent asked Brandy.

"Doesn't the fact that he did survive them answer that question?" Norm said.

"This is Lug Thompson," Daryl said, "one of the toughest sons of bitches to ever don a football uniform at our local college."

"What college?" Brandy said.

"The one close by," Dude said.

"I've seen him walk off shots to his head that

would bury mere mortals," Daryl said.

With a rasping groan, Lug sat up, lunging toward Brandy.

With a reactionary twitch, Trent fired Deputy Dibble's gun, shooting Lug just above the ridge of his eyebrow.

Lug plopped onto his back and was still.

"I don't think he's walking that one off," Norm said.

Brandy turned and looked at Trent. "Seriously? Give me that." She held her hand out for the gun. "Perhaps a woman should have that thing."

"I'll hold it," the brunette said.

"I've got it," Brandy said.

The brunette said, "Well you should at least clear the round in the chamber, and you might want to not hold it so close to the trigger safety there, see?"

Brandy looked at the gun in her hand, and then gave it to the brunette.

"Goody," the brunette said as she bounced on her heels.

"Is Luggy all right?" the blonde asked Norm.

"I'm going to leave that to the doctor," Norm said. He looked at Quint and winced, shaking his head.

Quint said, "Well the scarecrow lived without a brain."

"I did him a favor by putting him out of his misery, right?" Trent asked Quint.

Quint shrugged. "He was getting medical attention, he might've made it."

Trent said, "C'mon, he's missing an arm, his head is bashed in, and *he* shot him twice." He pointed at Dibble.

"Yeah, in the shoulder," Daryl said.

"But…I mean, the blood loss alone…."

"Shouldn't we, like, check his heartbeat again," the blonde said.

"Oh yeah," Brandy said, walking back toward Lug.

"I wuv you, Luggy," the blonde said. "We never had our chance, but I'll keep a lock of your hair always."

"He's bald," Norm said, "Where did you get a lock…ew."

"I never gave him a chance with me," the blonde said. "But now I realize—" She gasped and tapped on Dude's arm, pointing at the brunette. "Quick, get the camera. Great pic."

The brunette held the gun beside her face in a *Charlie's Angels* manner as she pouted her lips and lowered her eyelids. She then swung the barrel down and pointed it here and there, again as if posing for a 1970s exploitation film poster.

"Yay," the blonde cheered. "You look like Farah Waters."

"Fawcett?" Norm said.

"Yeah, like I said," the blonde said.

The brunette swung the barrel of the gun around again for another pose, and the rest of the group ducked out of the way, calling, "Whoa." The brunette hit her pose and then swung the barrel across them all again, causing them to duck and scatter. "Whoa." "Hey, stop."

The brunette stopped. "What?"

Brandy looked at her sternly and held out her hand.

"Fine," the brunette said and handed the firearm to Brandy. "It's not like it was chambered. I'm not an idiot."

"Did you hear that?" Norm said to Quint.

"I did," Quint said, raising the butt of his shotgun and gently thumbing back a hammer.

"I heard it too," Trent said. "Sounds like something is crashing through those woods."

"Hey, maybe it's Flash," Daryl said.

"Yeah," Dude said. "Hey, Flash, my man."

Daryl and Dude took off into the trees.

Deputy Dibble said, "Hey, I forgot there was still another student out here from the local college."

"Which coll—" Brandy began, but then said, "you know what, never mind."

"Should they be running into the woods like that?" Trent said.

"Nope," Quint said.

"There's probably a bear out there, right?" Trent said.

"Yup," Quint said.

Norm looked down at Burke. "Nothing from you?"

Burke looked away from him.

"Hey, Burke," Trent said. "No communiqué from the Squatch Warfront?"

"You said they don't exist," Burke said. "So you must be right. You're always right, aren't you?"

"Well, not always…some of the time…like probably sixty-five percent of the time? More like seventy maybe…seventy-five?"

"And you're sure those injuries to that boy weren't made by a squatch?" Burke said.

"Not all of them," Norm said.

"Shh," Trent said to Norm. He then said to Burke, "I'm pretty certain the blunt trauma was not made by a Bigfoot, yes."

"Seventy-five percent sure?" Burke said.

Trent turned toward Quint. "Quint, what's the odds those injuries were made by a bear?"

"About seventy-five percent."

"See?" Trent said to Burke. He then turned toward Quint. "Quint, what are the odds those injuries were made by a Bigfoot?"

"In real life?" Quint said.

"Enough said," Trent said.

Daryl and Dude trotted through the woods, calling out to Flash.

No response.

They stopped trotting and looked around.

"I don't see nothing," Dude said.

"Me neither," Daryl said. "We probably shouldn't get too far from the others, or we'll end up getting lost too."

"Yeah," Dude said. "I don't see him, we can head back."

"What do you think fucked up Lug like that?" Daryl said.

"Those guys shot him in the head."

"No," Daryl said, "what do you think ripped off his arm like that?"

"No clue, man, but that was way gnarly."

"Think it was a bear?"

"Maybe. Probably."

"Think it could be a Bigfoot?"

"Maybe if I was stoned I could believe that."

"You have any of your shit left?" Daryl said.

"Yup," Dude said, producing a joint. "Already rolled and everything." He lit it up and took a large toke. Coughing, he handed it to Daryl.

Daryl took a healthy drag and coughed. Between coughs he said, "Think it was a Bigfoot?"

"Sure," Dude said, taking the joint from Daryl, "why not?"

"So, you think that crashing we heard out here was actually Flash, or could it be something else?" Daryl said.

"Wouldn't have come out here if I didn't think it was Flash. What else could it be?"

"A bear?" Daryl said. "Maybe the one that fucked up Lug?"

"Nah," Dude said, coughing after taking another toke. He handed the joint back to Daryl and said, "Probably was Flash trying to reel in Lug. Lug probably gets himself hurt somehow, like he always does, and then takes off like an unmovable object. You know how Lug gets. That scrote almost came barging in on me and the girls. Almost blew the whole thing for me."

"If it was Flash out here then why didn't he answer when we called?"

"Probably scared Officer Barney will start shooting at him again."

Through coughs, Daryl said, "But it *could* be a bear we heard. *Or* the Bigfoot. And maybe it wasn't Flash at all."

Dude took the joint being handed to him, and said, "Whoa. So you think what we heard was the bear that tore off Lug's arm? Like it was chasing him, and now we're out here separated from everyone else while it is stalking us?"

"Precisely. Ever notice in horror movies, when people wander away from the main group, they get killed?"

"Whoa, yeah, then we should get back to the others."

"Yeah, no shit."

"I have to take a piss first," Dude said, pursing the joint in his lips and turning toward a tree.

"Good idea," Daryl said, joining him at the tree. "Be dumb to hold it until we got back to the safety of the others."

"Exactly. Bad for the bladder," Dude said as they peed. He then said, "Hey, our dicks look the same."

"First, they give us equal rights, and now this?" Daryl said.

The two began laughing.

Dude said, the joint still in his lips, "Nah, amigo, just saying glad I measure up."

Daryl craned his neck a little. "Not bad, white boy. We'll be calling you Bigfoot in these parts."

The two laughed again.

Dude said, "What if the Bigfoot has little feet? Would he still be a Bigfoot?"

The two broke into laughter while shaking free their final drops. They zipped up.

"You hear that?" Daryl said.

Daryl and Dude cocked their heads, listening.

"Argh, maybe it be the Littlefoot," Dude said, mocking Quint.

Daryl laughed harder. "You sound just like that old cracker. Guy is whack."

Dude took a deep toke and then held the joint out to Daryl, saying, "Arghhh—" trying to imitate Quint again through his coughing fit, when something, which looked to Daryl like a furry tree branch, swung from the forest.

Dude's head popped back like a Pez dispenser, his head dangling from the remaining sinew, his exposed throat leaking the smoke of his final toke like the barrel of a gunslinger's six-shooter.

"Dude," Daryl said, taking the joint from Dude's still extended hand, and then he ran.

———————————

"So let's get this all straight," Trent said. "It's a seventy-five percent probability that a bear killed Lug, and fifteen percent it was Dibble that killed him, and ten percent me?"

"I still think maybe you're the fifteen percent," Norm said.

"Fifteen percent is more, right?" Dibble said.

"I was thinking I'm more like five percent," Trent said. "Don't you agree?" he said, turning to Brandy.

Brandy shrugged and said, "I don't know, you did shoot him in the head."

"Quint, what's your vote?" Trent said.

"That I be hating math," Quint said.

"No," Trent said. "What's your vote about what killed Lug?"

"He be killed by a bear," Quint said.

"Thank you," Trent said.

"Still stupid to be shootin him in the face, though," Quint said.

"Was a squatch," Burke said in a muttered whine.

"Jesus not this again," Trent said. "We already went over this. We all agree it was zero percent a Bigfoot, right?"

They all muttered and nodded.

"Did you ever check again if he was dead?" Norm said to Brandy.

"Oh shit, yeah, I keep forgetting to do that, don't I?" Brandy said.

"You're just so smart, aren't you?" Burke said to Trent. "You and your—"

Daryl burst through the trees, never breaking from his run. "It wasn't Flash," Daryl said in a puff of smoke. He then continued up the path toward the campsite.

"Wait," Brandy called. "What was—?"

A growl erupted in the distance.

"Back to the campsite," Trent said.

"Rendezvous at the Alpha site," Deputy Dibble called.

The blonde and the brunette ran in the opposite direction.

"No, girls," Brandy said. "The other—"

Another growl rose from the trees.

"C'mon," Trent said, pulling Brandy with him toward the campsite.

Quint cocked the second hammer on his shotgun and squared toward the growls.

Norm struggled with Burke's wheelchair. "You know, you could be a little more cooperative here," he squawked at Burke.

"You go to the campsite," Burke said. "Leave me here."

"He choose now to be noble?" Quint said to Norm.

"You fucker," Norm grunted at Burke. "C'mon, we need to go."

"I want to embrace my fate," Burke cried. "Leave me here to face it."

Quint uncocked his barrels and grabbed one of the wheelchair's armrests. "What an asshole," he said. "Grab hold, laddie, we be running."

Norm grabbed the other armrest. Quint and Norm struggling to lift the chair, they ran along the path toward the campsite.

Chapter 8

Trent, Brandy, Daryl, and Deputy Dibble stood around the extinguished campfire of the campsite they'd only recently vacated.

"Why did we come back here again?" Brandy said.

"I was following him," Trent said, pointing at Daryl.

"The guy currently puffing away on a joint?" Brandy said.

"As a duly elected representative of—" Deputy Dibble began.

"Not now, Dibble," Brandy said.

"Sorry," Dibble said with a shrug.

"Are deputies elected?" Daryl said.

Brandy groaned.

Trent said, "Actually, maybe it's smart to fall back here. You know, an area we are familiar with, which is open, and we can see the bear coming."

"So we can watch it come and eat us?" Brandy said.

"Quint will just blast the thing with his shotgun. Isn't that why he's here?" Trent said.

"Quint isn't here," Brandy said.

Trent looked around in a sudden panic. "Where

is Quint?"

"And no Norm. Or Burke." Brandy said.

"That was no bear," Daryl said, taking a long haul off of the joint. Through a coughing spasm he said, "It was a Bigfoot."

"Christ," Brandy groaned.

"About what percentage, would you say—" Trent began.

"Enough of the percentages," Brandy said. "There is no Bigfoot."

"Maybe you should give the gun back to Deputy Dibble," Trent said.

"Yeah, I guess so," Brandy said. She handed the firearm to Dibble.

"I'll be more careful," Dibble said. "I promise."

Trent turned to Daryl. "So what did happen out th—"

A gunshot rang out as something broke from the trees.

"Jesus," Norm shouted as he and Quint broke through the trees, lugging Burke. "Dibble, will you please stop shooting that thing?"

After a stern look from Brandy, Dibble handed her the gun again.

"You really need to chill out, Dibble," Trent said.

Daryl offered Dibble the joint.

Dibble said, "As a duly elected—"

"Just smoke it," Trent said.

Dibble took the joint.

Norm and Quint set Burke down in the middle of the clearing. Quint then meandered along the perimeter of the campsite, watching through the trees.

"Where have you been?" Trent said to Norm.

"This asshole decided to suddenly sacrifice himself for the rest of us. Demanded we leave him behind," Norm said.

"And you didn't leave him?" Trent said.

"What do you think I am, that much of an asshole?" Norm said.

"No," Trent said, "Why didn't you leave him? You *should* have left him."

Brandy said to Burke, "You were really going to sacrifice yourself for us?"

"No, you idiots," Burke snarled. "I speak Sasquatch. I want to communicate with it. Ask it to take me with it so I can live the ways of the squatch."

Deputy Dibble coughed out smoke, and said, "You can talk to the Bigfoot?"

Norm, regarding the joint in Dibble's hand, said, "Did I miss something?"

"Can you tell the Bigfoot not to hurt us?" Daryl said to Burke.

"Guys, he can't speak Sasquatch," Brandy said. "There is no Sasquatch language. Primates don't just up and develop languages."

"Except for humans," Trent said.

"Except for humans," Brandy said.

"And other nonverbal communication used by gorillas, and chimpanzees, and orangutans," Trent said.

"True," Brandy said.

"And even baboons," Trent said.

"Yes, even those goddamn baboons," Brandy said. "Look, what I'm saying is, there is no primate language a person can just learn. It takes years of close interpersonal observations to learn to communicate with a primate, studying every tiny nuance of sound and movement just to decipher the simplest of meaning. There's no way he could—"

Burke started hooting and growling.

Brandy threw her hands in the air, saying, "And there he goes…."

"Is he talking Bigfoot?" Dibble said. "Or…" He looked at the joint in his hand. "I think this is making me go schizo."

"Oh, god," Brandy said, dropping her head into her hand.

Burke continued with his guttural sounds.

"Tell it to go away," Daryl said.

"Tell it we mean it no harm," Dibble said.

"That sound he be making is something a bear would investigate," Quint called from the far side of the site, still inspecting the forest beyond the tree line. "Might be good he stop."

Burke ignored everyone and only raised the volume of his grunting and hooting, his face turning red.

"That looks painful," Norm said.

"I think he's going to give himself an aneurysm," Brandy said.

"Or at the least shit himself," Trent said.

"Hey," Norm said, "have you noticed no one has

had to take a shit in the past two days? I know I haven't. No one's really eaten anything either. Weird."

"Will you stop doing that?" Brandy said to Burke. "You're going to attract the bear out there."

"Wasn't no bear," Daryl said. "It was like a…like a fucking Wookie or something. Like a fucking Bigfoot. And it killed Dude."

"Dude is dead?" Brandy said.

"Wait, was his name actually Dude?" Norm said.

"Thing knocked his head off with a vicious clothesline," Daryl said. "And so I ran and…hey, wait, I wasn't the first one killed. Maybe I'm not gonna—"

Something tore through the trees. It grabbed Daryl in a reverse headlock, lifting him off the ground.

Everyone scattered. Trent and Brandy darted behind a large fallen tree trunk. Dibble darted in front of a large fallen tree trunk. Norm tried wheeling Burke away, but Burke had engaged his chair's brakes. Norm struggled to unlock the brakes as Burke continued his Sasquatch calls. Quint, standing on the opposite side of the clearing, cocked a barrel and raised his shotgun, but he didn't fire, given he'd also hit the college quarterback.

The beast roared and spun, still holding Daryl in the headlock. When the beast stopped its spin, the momentum separated Daryl's head from his neck. Daryl's flailing body flew off—looking as if propelled from a jet of arterial spray—and struck Quint, knocking him over.

The beast looked down at the severed head still in its hands, seeming unsure what to make of it, and then tossed it into the air.

Norm caught the head. He regarded its frozen features—staring eyes and screaming mouth—which conveyed equal parts pain and terror. "Looks like I'll never sleep again," he muttered, tossing the head aside.

Burke continued hooting and growling.

Dibble continued puffing on the joint, which had all but burnt out.

The beast slapped its chest twice and held its hands to its ears.

"I'll be damned," Trent said.

"Um, I think that means it's going to attack, right?" Norm said.

Deputy Dibble threw the joint aside and burst into laughter, saying, "It already *did* attack."

Quint struggled to get Daryl's convulsing body off of him, the blood spraying him in the face like a slapstick bit involving a fire hose. "Where's the damn shotgun?" he shouted.

"The gun," Trent shouted at Brandy.

She began running toward Quint's shotgun, but Trent pulled her back.

"No," Trent said, "You have Dibble's gun."

Brandy took the gun from her waistband. "Is there like a safety on this thing or something?"

"How would I know?" Trent said.

"Because you already killed someone with it."

"Allegedly."

"The girl said a trigger safety," Brandy said. She then shouted, "Hey, Dibble, does this thing have a safety on it?"

"Fuck if I know," Dibble said, giggling.

"It's a Glock 9 mil," Norm shouted. "Just point and shoot."

Brandy pointed the gun, aiming at the wall of hair that was now strolling toward Burke and Norm.

"Please hurry and point and shoot," Norm said.

Brandy pulled the trigger, but it didn't work.

"The girl said something about chambered," Trent said. "Maybe try that sliding thing they do in the movies."

"Sliding thing?"

"You know…" Trent said, pantomiming racking the slide of a gun.

Brandy racked the slide and aimed again. With a piercing crack, the gun jumped in her hand. She fired three more times. The beast didn't drop, or stop, or even break stride.

"Why didn't it stop?" Brandy said.

"Could it really be bulletproof?" Trent said.

"Or maybe you're just a terrible shot?" Norm called. "Please try again."

Brandy lowered her brow in determination, imagining a bull's-eye on the beast, and pulled the trigger, but there was only a dull clicking from the gun.

"I think it's out of bullets," Brandy said.

"I was starting to think that thing would never run

out of bullets," Trent said.

The beast now stood over Burke and Norm.

About ten yards away, Quint finally got the still-convulsing body off of him and he searched for his shotgun.

Burke continued his hooting and grunting.

The beast regarded Burke and then cocked its head, like a dog hearing a command, a look of possible comprehension seeping into its eyes.

"What are you saying to it?" Norm said.

"That I hate you and it should kill you all," Burke said.

"What?" Norm squeaked. "Why would you tell it that?"

"Because I hate you. And I want it to kill you all," Burke said. He continued his hooting and grunting.

Quint found the shotgun. He raised it, hammering back the second barrel, but Norm was in his line of fire. He lowered the gun again.

The beast nodded, and then smacked its chest and raised its hands to its ears.

"Oh no," Norm said.

Burke said, "Oo-Oo-Hooey-Huey-Lewy-Garble-back. Kill them."

Norm closed his eyes and cringed.

The beast roared and lunged. It lifted Burke, wheelchair and all. Norm dove to the ground as the thing swung the chair around in a hammer-toss fashion, launching the chair and Burke through the air.

Quint raised his gun again, but he was bowled over as Burke's body landed on top of him. The shotgun landed several yards in the opposite direction. The wheelchair knocked over Deputy Dibble, landing on his ankle, the chair's wheel wedging against a fallen tree trunk, pinning Dibble's foot to the ground.

"Oh my god," Brandy said.

"Yeah, that was a 7-10 split," Trent said in awe.

Norm climbed to his feet, but stood frozen in the beast's gaze.

Trent said to Brandy, "Quick, throw the Glock to Dibble. He needs to reload it."

Brandy looked at the gun and then at Dibble. She cocked her arm back.

"Throw it hard enough so that it reaches him," Trent said.

"Are you fucking kidding me?" Brandy said. "Because I'm a girl, you think I can't reach him?"

The beast stood over Norm.

"Oh god," Norm said, withering like a plant in a deep freeze.

Quint struggled to get a flailing Burke off of him. Burke tried to hold Quint down, still hooting his Sasquatch calls.

"Throw it," Trent said to Brandy.

"Dibble," Brandy shouted and threw the gun.

Dibble turned toward her and caught the firearm between the eyes, knocking him out cold.

"Jesus," Trent said. "I said throw it to him, not *at* him."

"You said to—look, you're being an asshole—not roguish, but an asshole."

There was a sudden stillness as the beast regarded Norm, and then the thing touched Norm's shoulder. Norm's shoulder bounced back as if shoved by a bully, but still the gesture seemed almost gentle on the beast's part.

Norm opened his eyes and squinted up at the beast, which was now looking at him expectantly. Norm darted his eyes around in confusion before straightening a little out of his wither.

The beast touched Norm's shoulder again, and again, it regarded him expectantly.

Norm paused, and then hesitantly touched the beast on its thigh, feeling the coarse hairs—the texture of strands of hemp—upon his fingers.

The beast cocked its head questioningly, shrugged, and then strode off toward the unconscious Deputy Dibble.

"What was that about?" Trent said to Brandy.

"I don't know?"

"You're the primate expert. Expertize."

"Maybe it's something about the red shirt?"

"The red shirt *saved* him?"

"I don't know. Primates do see colors like we do. Perhaps through natural conditioning, it has learned to avoid the color red?"

"Either that, or maybe it felt sorry for Norm having to put up with Burke?" Trent said.

The beast now stood over the unconscious Dibble, looking at Dibble's pinned foot.

Brandy whispered, "Dibble, don't move."

"I don't think he's moving," Trent said. "You knocked him out pretty good."

"Don't start," Brandy said.

Burke called, "Gurgle-grump-oo-oo-ah-grimbot-growl. Kill them."

Quint shouted, "Get off me, you idiot."

The beast bent down and pulled the wheelchair from beneath the tree trunk. It then strode with it toward Burke and Quint.

Burke finally stopped flailing and turned to watch the squatch, like a child regarding an approaching parent.

Quint was able to buck Burke off of him and scrambled away, searching for the shotgun in the underbrush.

The beast stood over Burke again, cocking its head. Burke continued instructing it, in a series of hoots and grunts, to give him the wheelchair and then kill the others.

The beast nodded and swung the wheelchair down onto Burke's face. Burke's glasses were embedded deep into his brain, his eyes like squashed grapes against the broken lenses.

"Oh god, Burke," Brandy said from her vantage point, covering her mouth.

Burke's legs began to twitch and convulse as his brain fired off its final commands.

"Wait," Brandy said. "Was that motherfucker not really paralyzed?"

"Holy shit," Trent said in awe.

Quint still lurched around the underbrush looking for the shotgun.

Something burst through the trees behind Brandy and Trent, grabbing at them.

They both screamed in high falsettos.

Brandy glanced at Trent. Trent shrugged.

They then turned to see the warped face of Lug, his eyes staring dumbly in opposite directions, his jaw hanging uselessly from his skull, his nose concave rather than convex. He moaned like a bleating sheep in its death throes. Brandy and Trent scattered from behind the tree, running in opposite directions. Brandy's momentum brought her toward the Bigfoot.

The beast turned from Burke, its eyes locking onto Brandy. Brandy and the beast stared at one another for a moment before she muttered, "Oh shit."

Quint found his shotgun and he yanked at it from a tangle of ivy.

The beast bounded toward Brandy. Quint raised the shotgun's barrels, but before he could fire, the beast scooped Brandy up over its shoulder and bounded toward the deeper forest, smashing Lug in the face as it passed. As the beast disappeared into the trees, Brandy's rapidly fading voice shouted, "This is so demeaning."

Chapter 9

Trent and Quint ran to Norm, who remained frozen in place.

Dibble was still out cold.

Lug wandered around the clearing, continuing his moaning. His neck was dislocated by the last strike from the Bigfoot, and his head dangled flaccidly from his shoulders.

Trent asked Norm, "Are you okay?"

"Maybe you should tell me?" Norm said.

"You look to be fine," Trent said. "But why didn't that thing tear you apart?"

"Never seen anything like that," Quint said. "Like the creature be playing a game of tag with you."

Trent snapped his fingers.

"What is it?" Norm said.

"What's what?"

"You snapped your fingers like you've figured out some incredibly random thing you couldn't possibly have come up with so quickly," Norm said.

"Oh, yeah," Trent said. "I just realized…Rad Rocky's tag team partner…."

"Yeah?" Norm said.

"It was the Shanghai Samurai," Trent said.

"So?" Norm said. "What does that have to do with what just happened?"

"Well…I think it thought…you know…." Trent gestured to Norm like the connection should be obvious.

"Because I'm Asian, it thinks I'm the Shanghai Samurai? That's like really racist."

"We be talking about a giant monkey; I don't think it put that much thought into it," Quint said.

Norm said, "But Shanghai is in China, and samurai are Japanese."

Trent said, "Well it was the eighties, and I don't think wrestling promoters really cared about—"

"But I'm Korean."

"So was the Shanghai Samurai," Trent said.

"You're telling me it didn't kill me because I *am* a minority? Me being Asian *saved* me?"

"Animals don't be thinking like that," Quint said.

"But humans do," Trent said.

"You still think that's Rad Rocky?" Norm said, pointing emphatically in the direction the creature had gone.

"Doesn't what just happened prove it?" Trent said.

"That thing be no man," Quint said.

"Makes more sense than it being a Bigfoot, which doesn't exist," Trent said. "The steroids he was taking must have acted as some kind of rage serum. He's now Dr. Rocky and Mr. Rad."

"You put a lot of thought into that name, didn't you?" Norm said.

Trent shrugged, "When I was little I wanted to be… and out here in the woods, time on my hands and… yeah, maybe."

Quint said, "You know, we be wasting time while that girl still out there with that beast."

"That's right," Trent said. "So let's get moving."

"What about Dibble?" Norm said, pointing at the deputy, still crumpled on the ground.

Trent, Quint, and Norm gathered around Deputy Dibble. Lug wandered over toward them, still moaning through his obliterated jaw.

"Is he going to be all right?" Trent said.

"No," Norm said. "I don't know how it's even remotely possible he is breathing, never mind upright."

"Not Lug," Trent said. "Dibble."

"Oh. Oh, yeah." Norm kneeled beside Dibble. "He's got a pulse. He's breathing. I don't know if he's got, like, brain damage or something."

"How could you tell?" Quint said.

Trent picked up Dibble's firearm. "Check if he has any ammo," Trent said to Norm.

Norm checked the gun belt's magazine pouches. The first was filled with quarters.

"Did he expect a parking meter out here or something?" Trent said.

"Milk money," Quint said. "Boy won't leave home without it."

Norm checked the other magazine pouch. "Gum," he said, holding up a pack of Big Red. He stood and said, "And all this time I assumed the cinnamon was just his natural smell."

"You'd think with the amount this guy shoots that gun, he'd at least carry extra ammunition," Trent said.

The moaning Lug stumbled up to them, pawing at Trent with his only hand.

"Quit it," Trent said, shooing him away.

Norm counted on his fingers. "How many bullets were in that gun?"

"You'd have a better idea than I would; I didn't even know what kind of gun it was," Trent said.

"Some reporter," Norm said with a huff. He began counting on his fingers again. "Let's see, you used a round when you killed Lug—"

"Will you stop saying I killed him," Trent said. "He's right here…" He shooed the groping and moaning Lug away again, saying, "Will you quit it?"

"Then Dibble must have fired off like twenty shots," Norm said. "At least. How many bullets can fit in this thing?" He looked at the weapon's grip. "It's like a clown car."

Trent said. "Why even question things like that? Let it go. We have to save Brandy." He pushed Lug away. "Will you stop it?" He then said to Quint, "Shouldn't you like put this guy out of his misery?"

"That be murder," Quint said.

"What about the story you told us about Lucky in Nam?" Trent said.

"That was my friend," Quint said.

"That makes no sense," Trent said.

"I think it makes perfect sense, actually," Norm said.

"So what is the plan to find Brandy?" Trent said. "Jesus…" he said, ducking away from Lug, "he's like a damn mosquito." He turned Lug's shoulders. "Here, go see your buddy Norm."

"Huh?" Norm said.

"Quint, are you able to track that thing?" Trent said.

"Can try," Quint said. "But that thing has remained undetected for who knows how long, and these woods be large."

"So we just give up and let Brandy go?" Trent said.

"Nah," Quint said. "Didn't say I wouldn't try, just pointing out the odds. May be a way to get reinforcements first."

"We don't have time to head back to the sheriff's station for help," Trent said.

Norm, shooing away Lug, said, "But we have time for all these conversations?"

Quint said, "No need to be heading back to the station. There be a cabin about two klicks further in the woods. That cabin have it a ham radio. We go there and use that for our base of operations, plan our mission after calling in the cavalry."

Trent sighed and looked around the woods as if for more options. "I guess that's as good a plan as any," he said.

"Yeah, what could go wrong heading further into the woods?" Norm said.

"Do we take Dibble?" Trent said.

"Be a lot of extra weight," Quint said.

"Norm could push him in the wheelchair," Trent said.

"*Norm* can push him?" Norm said.

Trent shrugged. "Well, you *do* have practice and all."

"Safer he stay here," Quint said.

"He's safe here?" Trent said.

"I meant be safer for us," Quint said. "He might wake up." He turned and headed further into the woods.

Trent followed him.

"Stop that," Norm said, waving at Lug. "Stay," he said, like giving a dog a command. "Stay…hey, guys, wait up." Norm followed Quint and Trent into the woods.

———————————

They broke through the woods into a small clearing. A low, weathered wooden shack was nestled discreetly into the tree line.

"What is this place?" Norm said.

"I told you. A place with a radio." Quint said.

"Why are there so many barrels?" Norm said.

There were about a hundred barrels stacked on their sides in a massive pyramid. Beside it was a smaller shack with a black pipe jutting from its roof.

"They're aging barrels," Trent said. "This must be the Perfect Pitch distillery."

"Is this your place?" Norm asked Quint.

"I told you. I'm not the moonshiner. Just a customer."

They rounded the cabin to the front door.

Trent said to Quint, "Is there anybody here?"

"Yes and no," Quint said.

"Pretty much the exact answer I expected from you," Trent said.

"I think I just heard a banjo playing," Norm said.

"No one be playing banjos here," Quint said. He paused before opening the door. "What you see in here might not be a good look. You be taking a moment before getting all judgy."

A wave of rancid stench hit them as they entered the cabin.

"Holy Jesus…" Trent said, covering his mouth.

The air of the cabin buzzed, and Trent waved away several flies.

"Smells like something died in he—" Norm stopped when he saw the figure sitting in a chair in the center of the cabin. "Is that a corpse?"

"That be a corpse," Quint said.

They approached the figure, which was in an advanced state of decomposition. Although emaciated, it was very tall, with broad shoulders. The skin was a slick gray color, looking as if shrink-wrapped to a skull. The eye sockets were empty, the nose a shred of curling skin about to fall off. A toothy grin stretched across its face beneath its splitting black lips.

After a moment, Trent said, "How long do I have to wait before getting judgy?"

"Don't take you long, do it?" Quint said.

"I'd like to be judgy too," Norm said, covering his mouth with the bottom of his shirt. "What am I missing?"

Trent said, "You're missing the fact that, despite Quint having a copious supply of Perfect Pitch, the distiller has clearly been dead for some time, and Quint has been sitting on a dead body."

"Sounds uncomfortable and gross," Norm said.

"Not literally sitting on it."

"I know," Norm said, "Sometimes I can't help myself."

"Be just like you to jump to conclusions like that," Quint said to Trent. "But I said to stop and think it through. And not be so judgy."

"How does one not be so judgy when there's a corpse here?" Trent said. "And you knew about it. We're just over a mile from a major campsite. You couldn't contact someone about this?"

"If we're going to be judgy," Norm said, "then let's question why no one could find this moonshiner when he was just over a mile from a major campsite?"

"Did you kill this person, Quint?" Trent said.

"If I kill this man, why wouldn't I bury him out here in the middle of nowhere?"

"Are we really in the middle of nowhere?" Norm said. "You just said yourself—"

"I leave this man here for two reasons. One, to cover my ass. He be found, an autopsy will show he die natural. And second, he be my friend, and this be how he'd want to be left. Alone."

Trent shook his head.

"I can tell by your look that you still be judgy."

"I'm just going by what this looks like." Trent gestured toward the corpse.

"Are you sure it's a he? It looks a little like Ann Coulter," Norm said, regarding the emaciated corpse.

Trent glanced at the corpse, and then he did a double take. The body in the chair had strands of wispy blond hair flowing from its skeletal scalp. Trent then glanced around the room. The corpse was seated facing an old television set, the screen black for lack of power. Atop the television was a VCR, and atop the VCR were several tapes of MWSL Super Slam Championships. In the corner of the room Trent spotted a poster of Rad Rocky Hollywood plunging from the top rope, about to squash some poor schmuck lying on the mat.

Trent pointed again at the corpse, saying, "Wait a minute…is this…?"

"Rad Rocky Hollywood," Quint said. "Your supposed Bigfoot."

Trent stared at the corpse and then looked out the window as if at something in the distance. "That means…" he began to say, but stopped himself, as if unable to do the math of some impossible calculation.

Quint said, "It means that thing out there, it not be a wrestler, and it not be a bear."

"Which means…" Trent began but stopped, again as if unable to compute.

"It's really a sasquatch?" Norm said. "Then…if it isn't Rad Rocky, I'm not the Shanghai Samurai. Why didn't it kill me?"

Trent regarded the items of the room again. The poster, the videotapes, the television facing the window. He stared at the window a moment and then back at the television. "Do you think—"

"ColecoVision?" Norm said.

"Huh?" Trent said.

"What's a ColecoVision?" Norm said, reading the word off an ancient-looking gaming device attached to the television.

"He's got a ColecoVision?" Trent said, walking over to the television.

"This might be the most 1980s looking thing I have ever seen," Norm said, picking up the controllers.

"Aw, man. I loved ColecoVision," Trent said. "Everyone else had an Atari, but I had one of these. Way better graphics and—oh, it's got the Donkey Kong cartridge all ready to go. I was the best at Donkey…" his voice faded off. He picked up one of the VCR cassettes and regarded the picture on the box. It was a picture of Rad Rocky flying off the top rope, elbow pointed at the ground. He turned the box over and saw the picture of Rad Rocky hitting another wrestler with a folding chair. Norm joined him and the two inspected the photos on the back of the cassette boxes.

"Looks like that thing hitting Burke with his wheelchair," Norm said, nodding at Rad Rocky with the chair.

Trent then regarded a picture of Rad Rocky clothes-lining an opponent. Norm inspected Rad Rocky lifting a wrestler off the mat in a reverse headlock.

"You know, you're right," Norm said to Trent, "all the deaths *do* resemble Rad Rocky's moves, but if he's here dead, then…" he stopped and followed Trent's gaze to the window. "You don't think…?"

Trent handed Norm a box with a picture of Rad Rocky tagging the Shanghai Samurai into a match. "Do you have a better explanation?" He lined his arm up from the television to the window.

"You seriously think that Bigfoot thing sat outside the window and watched this guy reviewing his old matches on the television?"

"Brandy did say primates will mimic human behavior," Trent said.

"I don't remember her saying that," Norm said, handing Trent the game console's controller.

Trent looked at the game controller, his eyes traveling away on a mental time machine. "ColecoVision isn't ancient, by the way, and I'll kick your ass at Donkey Kong any day."

"We be needing to get that generator going," Quint said.

"Yeah, let's get this ColecoVision working; I am the Donkey Kong master," Trent said.

"No, you idiot, we be needing to get the radio up and running."

"Oh, that too, of course."

"I'm guessing the generator is outside?" Norm said.

"Be dumb to do otherwise," Quint said.

"So do we like draw straws as to who goes out?" Norm said.

"I be going out there," Quint said.

"No," Trent said. "Norm should go."

"What? Me? Are you nuts?" Norm said.

"You've got like…a shield," Trent said. "Like…a character shield or something."

"What the fuck is a character shield?" Norm said.

"The Bigfoot thinks it's the character of Rad Rocky Hollywood. And it thinks you're the character of the Shanghai Samurai. Being that character is like a shield against it."

"That sounds really convoluted," Norm said.

"All you have to do is let it tag you in, and don't tag it back. As long as you're tagged in, it won't do anything."

"Where the hell did you come up with that?"

"It's wrestling 101. As long as you run around like you're doing something, it has to stay off to the side. You just need to, like, run around and pretend to hit us or something."

"Oh, so you'll be out there too?"

"Of course," Trent said. "You distract it, Quint covers us with the shotgun, and I get the generator going."

"That not be a bad plan," Quint said.

"That not be a bad plan?" Norm said in a mocking tone. "You know, you sound like Yoda when you talk."

"Was that an insult?" Quint said.

"It's a terrible plan," Norm said.

"But you've got a character shield," Trent said.

"But what if I don't? How do I know that's why it didn't kill me? Or, what if it suddenly realizes I'm *not* the Shanghai Samurai? How do I know a character shield is even a real thing? Are you talking about plot armor or something? Because I think that's something different."

"Shh, lower your voice," Trent said. "Calm down."

"Calm down? You want me to waltz out there and play tag with a giant ape, and you're telling me to calm down?"

"Look, that thing might not even be out there. Which is why we all go and get the radio up and running so we can get help to find Brandy."

"But if that thing *is* out th—"

"Do you have a better plan?" Trent said.

Norm was silent and looked at Quint.

"You be a smart fella," Quint said. "Do ya have a better plan for us?"

Norm looked at the floor and said, "No. Your plan makes the most sense."

"Wouldn't go that far," Quint said. "But it be the plan with the most odds for success."

"Success for whom?" Norm said.

"For that girl that be whisked away," Quint said.

"All right," Norm said. "I'll do it."

Trent put his hand on Norm's shoulder and squeezed. "For Brandy," he said.

Norm nodded and said, "For Brandy." He looked at the two men and said, "Brandy needs to be rescued."

"Don't let her hear you say that," Quint said. "Or you be the one needing rescuing."

"All right," Trent said. "Let's do it. Quint, is the spare gas with the generator?"

"Oh no," Quint said, shaking his head. "There be no gas."

"Did you just say *there be no gas*?" Trent said. "The thing our whole plan hinges on, and there isn't any?"

"Generator doesn't run on gas," Quint said.

"Does it run on electricity?" Norm said.

"It runs on Perfect Pitch," Quint said.

"You're kidding," Trent said. "How potent is that shit?"

"One hundred and ninety-nine proof. Pretty much pure alcohol. Enough to run a generator."

"And one Vietnam Vet bear-hunter," Norm said.

"Is there even any left? Or did you clean it all out when Rad Rocky died?" Trent said.

"There be plenty left, wise ass," Quint said. "I think."

"You *think*?" Norm said. "You expect me to play tag with a giant ape while you try and find possibly nonexistent alcohol?"

"Do you have any left in your flasks?" Trent said.

"Not enough to be running that electricity."

"Can we do a blood transfusion between you and the generator?" Norm asked Quint.

"The generator will run the ColecoVision too, right?" Trent said.

"Still be going on about the damn—" Quint began.

"Forget it," Trent said, "we're wasting time. Let's go."

The three of them skulked from the house.

Trent put his hand on Norm's shoulder. Norm twitched, and Trent could feel the tremors beneath the kid's jacket. "It's okay," Trent said, "the beast most likely isn't even here."

"He's just off eating Brandy?" Norm said. "Is that supposed to make me feel better?"

"She's fine. It doesn't eat people."

"That we know of," Norm said.

Trent didn't respond. He removed his hand from Norm's shoulder so the kid didn't feel his own tremors.

Chapter 10

The air outside the cabin was still, the underlying silence accentuated by sudden bursts of birdsong.

Quint thumbed back the hammers of his shotgun, the sound ringing out loud as a thunderclap. He said to Trent, "That stack of barrels over there should be having the Pitch in them. The lower barrels probably be most likely full. There be a bucket and spigot in the shed there. Remove the barrel's cork and use the spigot to fill the bucket. Generator be in a cubby on the side of the house. Norm, you stay close by me. We be hunting."

Norm said, "I'm sorry, what did you say? I think I heard bucket and cubby."

"All you have to do is be the Shanghai Samurai," Trent said.

"*All* I have to do?"

"Hopefully you won't even have to do that," Trent said. "Thing probably isn't even around here." He glanced around at the trees, then said, "Good luck, gentlemen."

"You too," Norm said.

"Remember to prime the generator before starting her up," Quint said.

"Okay," Trent said.

"And you be careful," Quint said.

"Gee, thanks, Quint, that's kind of sweet," Trent said.

"Well, a girly-armed pissant like you needs to be taking extra caution so you don't get broke."

"Got ya, thanks," Trent said. He turned and ran for the shed.

Quint and Norm strolled into what could only be referred to as the cabin's yard. A more open area. The two men regarded the surrounding trees. Norm twitched at the sound of a songbird, his head darting around and his gaze settling on a tree.

"Is that an eagle?" Norm said.

"It be a cardinal," Quint said.

"Yeah, thought a red eagle was a little weird."

"Relax, son."

"Easy for you to say, carrying the giant gun."

"You be welcome to carry the giant gun."

"No thanks. I'd fuck it up. I don't want that on me."

"Exactly." Quint looked back toward the shed and the stacked barrels. "Where be that damn boy?"

With an echoing clank of tin, Trent emerged from the shed with the bucket and spigot. "Sorry," he said. "Kind of a mess in there. And I wanted to be sure I understood how the spigot works beforehand. I'm on it now." He waved awkwardly and then disappeared behind the barrels.

"And everyone be thinking he the smart one of the bunch," Quint muttered. He then turned to Norm. "Don't worry, son. You just be keeping your eyes peeled. And ears peeled, cause if it act anything like a bear, you be hearing signs of it before seeing it. Sounds be subtle, but they be there."

Trent's voice came from behind the barrels. "Damn it."

"What you be doing back there?" Quint said. "That bucket should be filled by now."

"I got it. I got it," Trent called. "Or, I will get it," he said.

"What that mean?" Quint said.

"Be meaning I be not able to get the cork out of the damn barrel," Trent snapped. "Who the fuck put these things in?"

"A roided-out professional wrestler?" Norm said.

"That explains it," Trent said.

"Idiot," Quint said under his breath, heading toward the barrels.

"How do I know this barrel even has anything in it?" Trent said.

"If it don't, then we be moving onto the next one," Quint said.

"There's like a hundred barrels here."

"Well, then we be checking a hundred."

"Seriously? This could take—"

Trent stopped when Brandy's voice rang out, "Norm, watch out."

Norm, who had been instinctively backing up toward the cabin during Quint and Trent's exchange, turned to find Brandy and the sasquatch on the top of the roof. The sasquatch leaned toward him, hand extended.

Quint snapped the shotgun's barrels up, but he paused.

"Brandy," Trent said, "you're alive."

"Why wouldn't I be alive?" she said.

"We thought that thing might've eaten you."

"Then where have you been?"

"We were coming up with a plan to rescue you," Trent said with a shrug.

"Do I look like someone who needs rescuing?"

"Um, kind of at the moment, yeah."

"I hate to interrupt, but why isn't Quint shooting the Bigfoot?" Norm said.

"Bad position here," Quint said. "Might hit you with some scatter shot. Don't think you want me to do that."

"You think right," Norm said, closing his eyes.

The sasquatch waited, hand extended.

"What is happening?" Norm said, his eyes still closed.

"It's waiting to tag you in," Trent said. "Get closer to it."

"No thank you."

"At least extend your hand," Trent called. "Let it tag you."

Norm squinted his eyes open and crept his hand toward the beast.

The beast tagged his hand.

Norm looked at his hand. Then looked at the expectant look on the beast's face.

"You've been tagged in," Trent called. "Do your thing."

"What thing?"

"You're the Shanghai Samurai; run around the ring. C'mon, you said you've seen Rad Rocky. Do that stupid wrestling shit. That thing won't hurt you as long as it thinks you're the Samurai."

Norm began running around the yard, waving his arms.

The beast climbed back up to the top of the roof, herding Brandy from the roof's edge, where she was trying to make an escape.

Quint lowered his shotgun again, lacking a clean shot. He noted a white armband on one of the beast's arms, and a pinkish one on the other.

Norm ran up to Quint and applied a weak elbow to his back. Quint turned his head and stared at him.

"Sorry," Norm said. "Just trying to make it look good." He ran off, shouting, "Shanghai Samurai." He bounced off a tree as if off the ropes, and ran toward another tree. He called, "I don't know how to feel about that thing thinking I'm the Shanghai Samurai—you know, the stereotyping and all—if it's offensive or beneficial, or…."

"It be a fucking Bigfoot," Quint said. "You be over-thinking it."

Norm bounced off the tree and headed toward Trent and the barrels.

Quint eyed Brandy's position relative to the beast, and then inspected the roof's overhang.

Trent just about had the cork out when he stopped and said, "It doesn't necessarily think you *are* the Shanghai Samurai. It is playing a role, and maybe assumes that you, being of Asian heritage, would *want* to play the role of the Samurai. In fact—"

"You got that cork out yet, you idiot?" Quint shouted.

"Oh, shit, yeah," Trent said. "Sorry, I just didn't want Norm to feel like—"

Norm slammed into the stack of barrels, pretending to splat against a wall. The barrels teetered.

"Crap," Trent said.

"Get out of there," Quint shouted.

Trent scrambled away from the barrels as the entire pyramid toppled over.

Norm stood beside Trent, and the two regarded the pile of barrels.

Norm said, "I guess a pyramid isn't the most stable structure."

"How am I supposed to know which are the full ones now?" Trent said.

"They're on the bottom?" Norm said.

"Bottom of what?" Trent said, waving his outstretched hands at the scattered barrels.

Quint called, "There be a hammer in the shed. Tap on the barrels and see which one not be hollow."

Trent looked at Norm and shook his head. "Why didn't he just have me do that in the first place?"

Norm shrugged.

"And what the fuck is he doing?" Trent said, gesturing toward Quint, who was now tucked beneath the eaves of the cabin's roof with his back to Trent and Norm.

"Looks like he's taking a piss?" Norm said.

"Are you taking a piss?" Trent called.

Quint waved at him in a *shut up* gesture.

Norm shrugged again. He then said, "Why is the Bigfoot wearing armbands?"

Trent shrugged and said, "Rad Rocky was known to wear sweatbands on his biceps?"

"I guess that would make sense, if—"

"Ahem," Brandy said.

The two men looked up at the roof and saw the beast and Brandy watching them, both with expectant looks on their faces.

Norm slammed his forearm into Trent's chest, knocking him over.

"What the—?"

"Shanghai Samurai," Norm said and ran off flailing his arms.

Trent watched him run off, then briefly spotted Quint skulking under the eaves, now looking like a teen trying to sneak back into his house after a night out partying.

Trent began to say, "Wha—?" but Quint waved him off again. Trent looked up to the roof. The beast still stood beside Brandy, watching Norm, but it also sniffed at the air.

Trent ran for the shed and grabbed the hammer. When he returned to the barrels, he spotted Quint peeking up over the edge of the roof at the beast and Brandy. Trent tapped on a barrel. It was hollow. He looked up and saw the beast staring at him. Its eyes narrowed, and it took a step in his direction.

Norm drove his shoulder into Trent's back, stealing his breath and knocking him down. They both then looked up at the beast, who looked to approve of the move.

"Shanghai Samurai," Norm shouted and ran off again.

Quint began tiptoeing along the side of the cabin, and Trent couldn't help but think just how much he looked like Elmer Fudd with that oversized gun. Trent looked up at the beast, then down at Quint again, sizing up the distance between them. He said, "You know—"

"Quiet, you idiot," Quint hissed.

"But—"

Before Trent could finish, the beast yanked Quint up onto the roof, gripping him in a bear hug, the shotgun pinned against Quint's chest.

Norm ran up to Trent.

"I thought you said it wouldn't attack as long as I'm tagged in," Norm said.

Trent gestured toward Quint as if in revelation of some inevitable fact. "Yeah, but Rad Rocky always cheated when someone wandered too close to the ropes. I was *just* trying to tell him to keep his distance.

But of course Quint has to think he knows everyth—"

Quint let out a screaming groan through gritted teeth as the beast squeezed him tighter in the bear hug.

"Quint," Norm shouted.

Quint's scream took on a gurgling sound.

"That's not good," Trent said.

"What do we do?" Norm said.

"I don't really know."

"It's killing him. What would the Shanghai Samurai do?"

"Well, Rad Rocky would grab the opponent who'd wandered too close and then throw him to the Samurai to be finished off." Trent shrugged. "That's all I got."

Norm ran to the most open portion of the cabin's yard. He waved his arms and then threw the karate chop flourish known as the Shanghai Dicer, adding in a few "Hi-yahs" for good measure.

"That's so racist," Trent said. "Maybe you should—"

"Can we not be doing that shit now?" Norm said.

"Okay," Trent said, and then muttered to himself, "Can we not be—? He's even starting to sound like Quint."

Norm gestured for the beast to relinquish Quint to the Samurai to be finished off.

After a final squeeze, which was accentuated with a crackle of ribs, the beast tossed Quint, shotgun and all, toward Norm.

Quint landed with a thud, letting out a wheezy grunt.

Norm knelt beside the grizzled hunter. Rivulets of blood crept from Quint's mouth.

Trent skulked from behind the barrels and walked toward them. When Trent saw Quint cough a mist of blood, he dropped the hammer and his walk became a sprint to their side.

Norm lifted Quint's head to give him a sip from his flask.

"He all right?" Trent asked, arriving beside them.

Quint coughed a spray of Perfect Pitch, tinged red with blood. Norm looked up at Trent and shook his head.

In a raspy voice, Quint said, "You be…getting that…son of a…bitch."

"We will, Quint," Trent said.

"Why do they call you Quint?" Norm said, tears spilling from his eyes.

The hunter smiled and wheezed, saying, "Because… I remind people of…a character in—" With that, the life ran from Quint's eyes.

"Character in what?" Norm said. "In *Jaws*?"

Trent placed his hand on Norm's shoulder. "C'mon, Norm, we have work to do."

"But do you think he was going to say *Jaws*?"

"Let it stay with him."

"But was it a secret, really? It has to be *Jaws*, right?"

"It's a mystery, whose solution will never be ascertained. The answer now dies with him."

"But—"

"Ahem," Brandy called.

Norm and Trent looked toward the shack's roof.

Brandy and the beast stood with their hands on their hips, both regarding the two men. Brandy called, "Remember me? I'd like to maybe move this on to the climax?"

"Move on to the climax?" Norm said.

"That's what she said," Trent said.

Norm arched an eyebrow.

"That's not a joke," Trent said. "It's seriously what she said."

"Today, please?" Brandy called.

Trent gestured to her and said, "You know, that roof isn't that high. Can't you climb down and run or something?"

"It won't let me," she said, gesturing to the beast. "And are you implying it's *my* fault that you have to rescue me?"

"No," Trent called. "It's not your fault we have to rescue you."

"What?" Brandy snapped. "So you're saying I *need* to be rescued?"

The beast dropped its head into its hand.

"Did that thing just understand us?" Trent said.

"I can't figure out half the shit that's going on right now," Norm said.

"Look," Trent said to Norm, "here's the plan. One of us will sneak up and try to get Brandy, while the other sneaks up on the thing with the shotgun. Which one do you want to do?"

"Neither?"

"Do you have any experience with firearms?"

"I've played Call of Duty."

"That'll do, I guess."

"That'll do? How is that better than you?"

"I told you, I've only been good at Donkey Kong."

"But you've actually used a firearm; you shot Lug in the face."

"Allegedly."

"Maybe you should do the gun thing."

"Fine. Then you'll go up to that thing and try to get Brandy?"

"No."

"We're running out of time," Trent said.

Trent and Norm looked up at the roof. Brandy and the beast both shrugged impatiently.

"Look," Trent said, "you have the character shield; you'll be fine. But you have to stay away from that thing because if it gets tagged back in, we're done for."

"Or at least you are. I'd technically still have the shield."

"Look, are you with me or are we just going to wait around for me to get squashed?"

Norm paused, then said, "Can I think about this for a moment?"

"Seriously?" Trent said.

"No, yeah, of course I'm with you. I was just trying to think up better, safer, options."

"This is the only option. You head toward the shed and try for a clean shot. I'll sneak over to the far side of the cabin and try to get Brandy. The second that thing notices me and turns away from you, unload both barrels."

"You want me to shoot it in the back?"

"Preferably, yes."

"I don't like that."

"What are you, John Wayne?"

"No…just doesn't seem right is all."

Trent and Norm looked at Brandy and the beast again. Brandy and the beast stared back.

"Do you have a better plan yet?" Trent said.

"No."

"Then, c'mon."

Norm held up the shotgun, inspecting the barrels. "Does this thing look bent to you?"

Trent inspected the barrels.

Norm added, "You're not going to offer a *that's what she said*?"

Trent arched his eyebrows.

"Not now?" Norm said.

Trent nodded, and after inspecting the barrel again, said, "I don't think it's bent. Maybe a little?"

"Can you fire a shotgun with bent barrels?"

"Sure," Trent said. "I'm sure it's fine. Ready?"

"No."

"Good. Let's go." Trent crept away in a commando crouch.

Norm opened his mouth to say something, but instead he snatched the flask from Quint's body and was off with shotgun in hand.

———————

Norm crept toward the shed, glancing at the shotgun as he went, trying to determine if it was truly bent.

Meanwhile, still in commando mode, Trent darted to the far end of the house. He eased into a position where he could see Brandy. She watched the beast watching Norm.

"Psst," Trent hissed. "Hey. Brandy."

Brandy twitched her head, looked around, and then spotted Trent.

"C'mon," Trent hissed, gesturing her toward him.

She shook her head and waved him away.

"Huh?" Trent whispered to himself. "What is she doing?" He then whistled to her and gestured again.

She waved him away again, and then her entire body stiffened.

The beast was looking at him.

On the other side of the house, Norm reached the shed and saw the beast turning toward Trent. The beast's back was now exposed to him. He cocked both barrels and raised the gun, his focus zeroing in on the wide back of the giant primate. His hands began shaking. He lowered the shotgun.

The beast didn't move as it regarded the journalist, but then it thudded its chest twice and raised its hands to its ears.

It was now or never, and Norm thought, *what would Quint do?* Remembering the flask he'd taken from Quint's body, he twisted off the flask's cap and took a swig.

As Trent watched the beast do Rad Rocky's signature calling card, he knew he was done for. Should he run, or should he wait for the beast's inevitable attempt at a body slam and try to avoid it?

The beast tensed its legs, about to spring, but it was interrupted when Norm began shouting, "Oh, god, I can't see. I can't see. That Perfect Pitch made me blind."

The beast's head snapped toward Norm. It then grabbed Brandy and hopped from the cabin's roof to the roof of the shed. It placed Brandy on the shed and then jumped down to the ground. It watched Norm flailing around, the barrels of the shotgun waving about in random directions like beach grass in a gale.

"Norm, careful," Brandy shouted.

"Everything is so blurry," Norm said. "Should I take the shot?"

"No," Trent and Brandy both shouted.

The beast watched Norm flail about.

Trent knew it was time to act; he needed to get Brandy. He ran for the shed.

"No. Look out," Brandy shouted.

The beast snatched a barrel from the toppled pile and threw it at Trent. Trent ducked the barrel, losing his balance for a moment, but he recovered and continued running toward the shed.

The beast threw another barrel, this one bouncing off the ground and then rolling toward Trent. Trent hopped over the barrel, barely clearing it, and tumbled to the ground. As he scooted to his feet, he spotted the hammer he'd dropped earlier. He snatched the hammer up and ran toward the beast. Waving the hammer over his head, he screamed the call of a warrior as the beast threw another barrel.

Trent gripped the hammer tight, wielding it like Mjölnir itself, intent on smashing that barrel and getting Brandy to safety. The barrel was upon him, and he swung the hammer. With a hollow thud, the hammer bounced off the wood and caught him squarely in the face, dropping him in a heap.

"Trent," Brandy screamed.

Norm raised the shotgun and aimed.

"Wait," Brandy shouted. "I thought you were blind."

"I can see much better now," Norm said.

"Do not shoot," Brandy screamed.

But with that, a loud crack rang out. The beast dropped to the ground and was still.

"I said don't shoot," Brandy shouted.

"He didn't," Sheriff Vance said, holstering his .357 Magnum.

"C'mon, now," the sheriff said, helping Brandy down from the shed.

"Thank you, but…." she said.

"*But?*" the sheriff said.

"Did you have to kill it?"

"Um, yes," Norm said, arriving beside them and looking down at the beast. "Although it was kind of anticlimactic the way it happened."

"You can see?" Brandy said to Norm.

"For the most part. Little blurry, but I can see that that thing is dead."

"It's just that…" Brandy's voice trailed off as she looked down at the beast at her feet. "Amazing animal. Clearly not bulletproof though."

"And I guess it doesn't dissolve when it dies," Norm said.

"Bulletproof? Dissolves?" the sheriff said. "What are you talking about? Have you been listening to that Burke guy?"

"Nah," Norm said. "Why'd we listen to that idiot?" As he said this, he swung the shotgun, gesturing in the direction of the campground where they'd left Burke's body.

"Whoa. Why don't I hold that thing?" Vance said, nodding at the shotgun.

"Thank you, yes," Norm said, handing it over to him.

"How did you find us?" Brandy said.

"Melody and Vivian came running out of the woods and told me you all were in trouble," the sheriff said.

"Melody and Vivian?" Norm said.

"Blonde and brunette college girls? They said they were with you."

"They made it out of the woods without getting lost?" Brandy said.

"Yeah," Sheriff Vance said. "Apparently they'd tied ribbons to the trees like breadcrumbs leading their way back. They're clever girls."

"That adjective never crossed my mind while talking to them," Norm said.

"Yeah, well, their getting out of these woods saved you. And Deputy Dibble. And their friend Lug."

"Lug's still alive?" Brandy said.

"Looks like he'll pull through."

"So…" Norm's voice trailed off, then he said, "That explains how you knew we needed help, but how did you know to find us here? I thought you'd never been able to find this distillery?"

The sheriff flicked his eyes away for a moment, then flicked them back onto Norm. He pointed the shotgun at Norm and Brandy, thumbing back the hammers. "Well, Mr. Yoo, I wish you hadn't asked that."

"What?" Brandy squealed.

"I guess that's an interesting enough twist," Norm said.

"Why does there have to be a twist?" Brandy said.

"There's always a twist; I knew there had to be one coming," Norm said. "Killing the Bigfoot was way too easy."

"You're right, Mr. Yoo," Sheriff Vance said, "it was easy, but you had to complicate things, and now I need to simplify them again."

"But why?" Brandy said.

"Because the Perfect Pitch Empire is that valuable," Vance said.

Norm looked around at the shabby cabin and property. "Can you really call this an empire?"

Brandy said, "You're going to kill us because you want some shitty moonshine operation?"

"Something like that, yes. Now it will finally be mine."

"Why now?" Brandy said.

"Because now I can move in without the opposition," Vance said.

"Opposition? Rad Rocky looked to be dead for a while," Norm said.

"But his protective beast was not."

"The Bigfoot?" Norm said.

"It wouldn't let me anywhere near the place," Vance said.

"Why didn't you just shoot it in the head?" Norm said. "Seems to have worked."

"I was under the impression it was bulletproof."

"I thought you didn't know anything about it being bulletproof?" Brandy said.

"I was bullshitting you."

"Then why did you just shoot it now?" Norm said. "Didn't you still think it was bulletproof?"

"Thanks to Brandy here, I now know that it is not."

"Me? Why thanks to me?" Brandy said.

"Because I see the bandages on the beast's arms, and I assume it's because it was injured. And, despite you being its prisoner, you as a primate lover, would have tended to its wounds. Ironically, it was your kindness that led to its death."

"Seems like a flimsy reason to think you could kill it all of a sudden," Norm said.

"I didn't bandage anything," Brandy said.

"But the bandages on its arms," Vance said.

"That wasn't me," Brandy said.

Vance looked off, pondering for a moment. "Then I guess it bandaged itself. Must have found Mel and Vivian's ribbons."

"I thought the armbands were just part of its wrestling outfit," Norm said.

"Wrestling outfit?" Vance said. "What are—?"

"It's a long story, and why are we even having this conversation?" Norm said. "I mean, why are you telling us your entire plan if you're just going to kill us?"

"I don't know," Vance said. "But you're right. Say goodbye."

"Norm," Brandy whined, spreading her hands and shaking her head. "What are you doing?"

"What? It's a legitimate question," Norm said. "He could have killed us like ten minutes ago. He keeps yapping."

"Well I'll rectify that now," Vance said. He lifted the shotgun. "And I will kill you with Quint's shotgun, no less, which you, Norm, were kind enough to hand over to me. Now I don't have to use my own weapon, and I can say it was Quint that killed you and—"

"See? He's doing it again," Norm said.

"It is kind of annoying," Brandy said.

"Fine, say goodbye," Vance said, aiming the shotgun.

With a roar, the sasquatch leapt from the ground to block the shotgun's blast.

Vance pulled the trigger. The gun blew up in his hand, buckshot exploding backward, tearing through the flesh of Vance's face and throat. With skin hanging from his skull in bloody skin streamers, Vance stared dumbly at the shotgun still in his hands. Then the look of realization dawned in his eyes, and he dropped to the ground.

In the ensuing silence, with a thick white fog of spent gunpowder hanging about their shoulders, everyone, including the sasquatch, pondered the outcome.

The sasquatch turned toward Brandy with a questioning look in its simian eyes.

Brandy shrugged and shook her head. "I don't know," she said to it. She then turned to Norm and said, "What happened? It's like the gun just exploded in his hands."

"Yeah, that was weird…" Norm said. He then snapped his fingers. "Oh, wait, I forgot. The barrels of the gun were bent. I guess I'm glad I didn't shoot the Bigfoot in the back after all."

The sasquatch cocked its head and raised one of its eyebrow ridges.

Norm shrugged. "Hey, sorry, but you know, the whole saving the girl thing."

"No one needed saving," Brandy said.

"Well," Norm said, "You were—"

"I said no one needed saving, Norm," Brandy growled. She then turned to the beast. "You jumped in front of us to block the bullets."

"I think it might actually be called buckshot," Norm said.

"Quiet, Norm," Brandy said. She then turned to the beast. "You stopped the sheriff from killing us."

"Well, technically, the gun would still have blown up in his hands anyway," Norm said.

Brandy smacked Norm on the arm with the back of her hand. She said to the beast, "You saved us."

"I thought you didn't need savin—ung." Norm doubled over as Brandy smacked him again, this time in his testicles. "Okay," he gasped.

Brandy said to the beast, "Thank you. You are truly our friend. And…MWSL Super Slam Champion?"

The sasquatch straightened proudly. It then slapped its chest twice and raised its hands to its ears. It pumped its fists over its head before holding out a palm vertically toward Brandy.

"What?" Brandy said. "Like a wave?" Brandy held up her hand and waved it. "I'm not sure what you're doing there," she said.

Norm, still doubled over, croaked, "It wants a high five."

"Oh," Brandy said with a giggle. She high fived the beast.

The sasquatch then held its hand up toward Norm. Norm didn't move.

"High five the Bigfoot, Norm," Brandy said.

Still bent over, Norm said, "I don't think so."

"High five the fucking Bigfoot, Norm."

"Okay, okay," Norm said, holding up his hand. "But he better not be tagging me in or anything; I'm done being the Shanghai Samurai."

The sasquatch high fived Norm, and with one more pump of its fist, it ran off into the woods.

Brandy, watching the sasquatch run off, wiped a tear from her eye.

Norm said, "It would appear that beauty truly did tame the—"

"Fuck off."

"Right."

Brandy bent down over Sheriff Vance.

"Is he definitely dead?" Norm said. "I mean, wouldn't surprise me if he suddenly leapt up."

Brandy checked his pulse and peered into the holes shredded through his face. She picked up a thin stick and poked it into one of the holes, pushing the stick down with a squishing sound until it hit the ground below his skull. "I don't think he's getting up."

"I'd still maybe back up," Norm said. "You know, given how the day's gone."

Brandy stood, regarding the sheriff for one final moment. "Who'd have thought someone looking so much like Denzel could be such an asshole?"

"I guess Donkey Kong ain't got shit on him."

"Yeah," Brandy said. "I have no idea what you're talking about."

"I was referencing the line in—"

"I don't really care," Brandy said, her voice thick with exhaustion.

They looked around the woods in silence for a moment, allowing the birds' calls to intensify the silence.

"So…" Brandy said and shrugged. "I guess we try and find our way out of here?"

"Maybe we should check on Trent?" Norm said.

"Oh my god, Trent," Brandy squealed and ran over to the fallen journalist.

"Is he alive?" Norm called to her.

She checked for a pulse. "Yes," she said.

Trent returned to consciousness with a groan. He opened his eyes, which were both black. His nose was crooked.

"Are you okay?" Brandy asked him.

He blinked and shook his head slightly to clear away cobwebs, then nodded.

"Your face," Brandy said. "I think you might have broken your nose." She grinned. "Hopefully that roguish smile is all right," she said.

He opened his mouth in a bloody toothless grin.

"Whoa, ew, okay, we can work on that," Brandy said. She called over her shoulder, "Hey, Norm, think you can get that generator running so we can radio for help?"

"Or we could use the sheriff's walkie talkie?" Norm said.

"I'm okay," Trent said, climbing to his feet with a grunt. "I can walk."

"Here, lean on me," Brandy said, the two beginning to walk with arms around each other's shoulders.

"But maybe we should, like, get help and…" Norm said.

"I feel like walking," Trent said.

"But…" Norm said, watching the two walk off as the sunset's dying light blared through the tree branches. "Whatever," he said, turning back and snatching the sheriff's flashlight. Before he joined the others, he made sure a folded piece of paper was still in his pocket. The recipe for Perfect Pitch, which he'd snatched from Rad Rocky's kitchen table. "Hey, wait up," Norm called.

In the distance something hooted. It could have been an owl. It could have been a wolf. It could have been the new MWSL Super Slam Champion.

But it was probably an owl.

Coming Soon

From STONE Pulp Press

Vincenzo Longhorn is coming for your wife.

No Ire

By: Carver Cane

Read Chapter 1 here:

She was a woman in her forties, but could take any man from zero to a hundred in no time at all. He was Vincenzo Longhorn, the man whose epic member—featured on covers of VHS tapes found under counters and in secret rooms of 1990s video stores—could stop a girl cold. They sat in the partial shadows of a back booth. The one furthest from the bar and the front entrance. The kind of booth with the wrap-around seat. A place to hide and scheme. A place to hate. And a place to love. They were doing it all.

"It's so big," She said.

"Twelve lethal inches of power," he said.

"I thought it was bigger."

"That's pretty freaking big."

"It's so hard."

"Wouldn't really work if it wasn't," he said.

"Is it ready and loaded?"

"Always is. Just waiting for you to tell me what you want me to do with it."

"You know what I want," she said. Leaning closer to him, closer to it. She glanced away and then said, "Here comes the waitress, get it off the table."

With surprising quickness, Vincenzo slid the impressive weapon off the table, returning it between his legs.

The waitress stopped beside their table and eyed them suspiciously. They didn't know she eyed everyone suspiciously; after all, only suspicious people came into that bar. And as for the back booth, the only people who sat there were guilty as hell. She grimaced, seeing the man's hands below the table, remembering that the Mexican kid who usually mopped up the blood and semen left behind each night had disappeared. Now it was up to her to do it, and she contemplated asking Big Hal for the extra two dollars an hour he'd paid the kid. But not being sure if it was the ICE that made the kid disappear, she kept her mouth shut.

"Another round of drinks?" the waitress asked.

"Yes, please," the woman sitting at the table said. Her eyes glinted like light off hot, polished steel, and her pressed smile hid secrets only the devil could deduce. "Another martini," she said.

The waitress eyed the man, not realizing she was eyeing porn royalty. Not realizing what was held below that table. "You?" the waitress said to him.

"Yeah," he said.

"Another water?" the waitress said, as if questioning his manhood. If she only knew.

"Soda water," the man corrected. "With a twist," he added.

The waitress smirked and walked away, her hips wagging like a scolding finger.

The woman at the table turned back to Vincenzo, her eyes like animals looking to devour him. "Can I see it again?"

"She'll be back soon," he said, nodding toward the waitress.

The woman reached under the table and began caressing the hard steel. "Tell me what you're going to do with this again," the woman said, her voice laced with desire.

"Tell me what you want me to do with it," he said.

"You *know* what I want," she said, leaning forward, brushing her lips against his.

"I'm not sure I do," he said.

"Then maybe I heard wrong about the great Vincenzo Longhorn."

"Depends what you heard."

"I heard he knew how to use this thing. But maybe you're no longhorn after all."

"The longhorn is accurate."

"Maybe what you thought was a longhorn was nothing but an udder." The weapon twitched under the table. She gripped it tighter. "Maybe instead of Vincenzo Longhorn, you should be called Bessie the Milking Cow?"

"Stop it."

"Bessie the Milking Cow starring in *Udder Desire*?"

"Do you want me to get mad?" he said.

"Maybe," she said.

"Then, *enough*," he hissed.

The waitress returned and set their drinks on the table. When the man and woman at the table didn't acknowledge her, the waitress walked away, her wagging hips now a middle finger.

Vincenzo and the woman stared at one another. His expression heated almost to a rolling boil. Her expression smooth as ice.

She let go of the weapon between his legs and said, "Let me see it again."

"You don't deserve to," he said.

"Deserving is subjective," she said.

"I thought deserving is the reason we're here."

"There are those who deserve satisfaction," she said.

"And those who deserve denial," he said.

"Do I really deserve more denial?"

"I think maybe you're confusing deserve with desire."

"Are you going to deny me my desire for satisfaction?"

"Do you deserve that satisfaction?"

"Do I deserve my desire for satisfaction?"

"Hold on, do you deserve the denial of satisfaction, or do you deserve the satisfaction of what someone else deserves?"

"I'm not sure I follow. Who is the someone else who deserves something?"

"I thought we were talking about your husband?"

"My husband? How did he get into this?"

"I thought we were talking about you deserving your desire of the satisfaction of getting what your husband deserves?"

"*I* get what my husband deserves?"

"No, he gets what *he* deserves."

"I deserve for my husband to get what he deserves?"

"Yes."

"Then, yes."

"Wait, you're saying yes to…?" He stopped, looked at the ceiling, and then said, "Look, do you want me to kill your husband or not?"

"Yes," she said, caressing the weapon beneath the table. "Now can I see it?"

He shifted, pulling the weapon from between his legs.

"What is it called again?" she said.

"It's a .44 Magnum, baby, like the one Dirty Harry used."

With a flash of gunmetal, the weapon was almost on the table again when she stayed his hand. "Here comes the waitress again."

As he hid the weapon under the table again, a loud clap of thunder filled the bar.

Vincenzo and the woman looked at one another as a wisp of white smoke wafted from beneath the table, and Vincenzo said, "I think I might've just shot my dick off."

"Seriously? Your dick again?"